John Wesley, Charles Wesley, W. E Dutton

The Eucharistic Manuals of John and Charles Wesley

reprinted from the original editions of 1748-57-94. Second Edition

John Wesley, Charles Wesley, W. E Dutton

The Eucharistic Manuals of John and Charles Wesley
reprinted from the original editions of 1748-57-94. Second Edition

ISBN/EAN: 9783337251499

Printed in Europe, USA, Canada, Australia, Japan

Cover: Foto ©Andreas Hilbeck / pixelio.de

More available books at **www.hansebooks.com**

THE

Eucharistic Manuals

OF

JOHN AND CHARLES WESLEY.

Reprinted from the Original Editions of
1748-57-94,

EDITED, WITH AN INTRODUCTION, BY THE

REV. W. E. DUTTON,

VICAR OF MENSTONE.

SECOND EDITION.

JOHN HODGES,

KING WILLIAM STREET, CHARING CROSS, W.C.
1880.

CHISWICK PRESS:—C. WHITTINGHAM, TOOKS COURT
CHANCERY LANE.

CHISWICK PRESS:—C. WHITTINGHAM, TOOKS COURT
CHANCERY LANE.

TABLE OF CONTENTS.

INTRODUCTION.

THE republication of the Sacramental Hymns, and other Eucharistic Manuals of John and Charles Wesley, has become almost a necessity of the times. It has been often asserted of late that the Wesleys held opinions, and taught doctrines far in advance of the times in which they lived, and very different from those taught by so-called Wesleyans of the present day.

With reference to the doctrine of the Holy Eucharist, it seems to me that the Manuals now republished ought at once, and for ever, to settle the question.

The "Companion for the Altar" was first published in the year 1742, and recommended for general adoption. In its separate form it passed through many editions, and it was also included in the "Christian Pattern," which was very extensively used as a book of devotional reading by the early

Methodists. That Wesley constantly urged its use as a standard devotional work, his Journals and the Minutes of Conference testify; nor am I aware that he ever repudiated any of its doctrines.

The case is much stronger as regards Dean Brevint's Treatise on the Christian Sacrament and Sacrifice; for it was deliberately adopted as a clear and concise statement of Wesley's own teaching, republished as a preface with every edition of the Hymns, and stood forth to the world for half a century as the authorized standard of Methodist teaching, upon this most important and vital doctrine. Wesley's latest biographer, himself a Methodist preacher, acknowledges that there can be no doubt that Wesley, by publishing this extract from Brevint, made it his own.[1]

The first edition of the "Hymns on the Lord's Supper" was published three years later than the "Companion for the Altar," and sold so rapidly that nine successive editions were exhausted during Wesley's lifetime, and a tenth was published three years after his death. The book has now been out of print for many years, and is little known, either among Methodists or Churchmen; hence the necessity for its reproduction.[2]

It is necessary to notice that the names of J. and C. Wesley appear upon the title-page of every edition, because a somewhat discreditable attempt is now

---

[1] Tyerman's "Life and Times of Wesley," vol. i., p. 501.
[2] Since the first edition of this book, the Hymns on the Lord's Supper have been republished amongst the collected poems of John and Charles Wesley.

being made by those most interested to fasten the responsibility of the Hymns upon Charles Wesley alone; for it is alleged that he was not so much the exponent of Methodist theology as his brother John. How far this latter assumption may or may not be true, is beyond the range of our present inquiry; but there is no reason for supposing that John Wesley wished to be relieved from the joint responsibility attached to this volume, or that Charles therein advanced a sentiment which was in the least degree distasteful to his brother. On the contrary, the book was always published in their joint names, and always sold at all the preaching-houses in town and country. When, upon one occasion, *e.g.*, in " Hymns and Sacred Poems," Charles did write sentiments repugnant to his brother, John publicly repudiated them, and disclaimed all responsibility in their publication.

Nor is there anything in the Hymns contrary to the teaching on the same subject in the sermons and other doctrinal statements of John Wesley. But as the contrary is stated, I purpose in this inquiry to give a very brief analysis of the book before us, and see how far it agrees with other acknowledged writings. And here I may observe that the Hymns are not merely a poetical version of the Treatise by which they are prefaced, but in many cases they develop the thoughts more fully, and state the doctrine more clearly. I will give one illustration of this in passing : " As the Israelites whenever they saw the cloud on the Temple, which

God had hallowed to be the sign of His Presence,
presently used to throw themselves on their faces,
not to worship the cloud, but God; so whenever I
see these better signs of the glorious mercies of God,
I will not fail both to remember my Lord who appointed them, and to worship Him whom they represent."—*Treatise*, p. 77.

This is the poetical comment:—

> " To Thee this Passion we present
>   Who for our ransom dies;
> We reach by this great instrument
>   The Eternal Sacrifice.

*   *   *   *   *   *

> The Lamb His Father now surveys,
>   As on this Altar slain,
> Still bleeding, and imploring grace
>   For every soul of man."   *Hymn* cxxvi.

> " Did Thine ancient Israel go
>   With solemn praise and prayer
> To Thy hallow'd courts below,
>   To meet and serve Thee there?
> To Thy Body, Lord, we flee;
> This the Consecrated Shrine,
> Temple of the Deity,
>   The real House Divine."   *Hymn* cxxvii.

And now to proceed with our analysis.

I. The Holy Eucharist is first a memorial of the
sufferings and death of Jesus Christ, wherein is
represented all the stripes and bruises which He
endured;[1] wherein His death is set forth;[2] and

---

[1] Hymns ii., iii.   [2] Hymn xviii.

Jesus is presented before God, and before man, as still bleeding and suffering for mankind.[1]

II. But it is not merely as a bare memorial, or an empty sign, that we perpetuate this mystery,[2] but as a Commemorative Sacrifice,[3] in which our Saviour is really and truly present;[4] and the Sacrament of the Altar, by commemorating and representing the actual bloodshedding upon Mount Calvary, becomes a Bloodless Sacrifice, pleading before God all the merits of .that Great Sacrifice, as effectually as Christ Himself pleads before the Father's throne in heaven.[5]

III. This Holy Sacrament is not only a Commemorative Sacrifice, but a Feast conveying blessings to man, nurturing and sustaining his soul; it is the divinely appointed means of access to God, the channel through which His graces are given. To this Feast all Christians are invited to meet their Saviour, and to feed upon His precious Body and Blood, which once having given for the life of the world, He there offers to be the sustenance of every faithful soul.[6] It is a sure instrument of present grace, and the only safe pledge of our everlasting inheritance.[7]

IV. Assisting at this great Sacrifice we unite ourselves to God, and the sacrifice of our person and goods is only acceptable when joined with this. It

---

[1] Hymn v.
[2] Hymn lxxxix.
[3] Hymn cxxiii.
[4] Hymns xxxix., cxvi.
[5] Hymn cxvii.-cxxvi.
[6] Hymn liv.
[7] Hymns xciii.-cxvi.

unites us also to all the saints who have gone before,[1] and thus we bear a part in that perpetual sacrifice of praise and thanksgiving which has been continually ascending from earth to heaven ever since our Saviour suffered upon Mount Calvary.[2] Therefore this Sacrifice should be offered daily in thankful commemoration of our Saviour's death, and in loving obedience to His commands. Because we have neglected to do this, the Church has lost her power over the hearts of men; her glorious places have become desolate, and her once flourishing sanctuaries laid waste. Dogs, and swine, and heathen profane her holy places, and trample under foot her precious jewels. But when she returns to the fulness of her first love, and the " pure primeval flame " glows in the bosom of her children ; when the " Daily Sacrifice " is once more offered upon her altars, then Christ will bring His Spouse the Church out of the wilderness, washed from every spot and wrinkle, made perfect in grace, and " meet for the joy which ne'er shall end." [3]

In accordance with these sentiments, Wesley never failed to impress upon his followers the absolute necessity of being present at, and receiving, the Holy Sacrament, if they would flourish in grace, enjoy the fruits of Christ's kingdom upon earth, and prepare themselves for the enjoyment of His everlasting kingdom in heaven. Many extracts might

---

[1] Hymn xcvi.   [2] Hymns cxxviii.-cxlviii.
[3] Hymn clxvi.

be given to prove this, and I purpose calling atten-
tion to a few.

1. First, as to the benefit and grace of the Holy
Eucharist. I need scarcely do more than give a
summary of Wesley's sermon "On the Duty of Constant Communion." And I do this the more readily
because it will illustrate other points I have men-
tioned, and we have his own authority for saying
that this sermon embodied the doctrine which, upon
this subject, he had consistently preached for fifty-
five years. In this Sermon, he says—

"It is the duty of every person to receive the
Lord's Supper as often as he can, because (*a*) it is
a plain command of Christ. This appears from the
text, 'Do this in remembrance of Me:' by which, as
the Apostles were obliged to bless, break, and give
the Bread to all that joined with them in these holy
things, so were all Christians obliged to receive
those signs of Christ's Body and Blood. This command was given by our Lord, when He was just
laying down His life for our sakes, and is therefore
His dying command.

"(*b*) The benefits of receiving the Holy Communion are (1) the forgiveness of our past sins, and
(2) the present strengthening and refreshing of our
souls. The grace of God given herein confirms to
us the pardon of our sins, and enables us to leave
them. Christ's Body and Blood is the food of our
souls; it gives strength to perform our duty, and
leads us on to perfection. Whosoever, therefore,
goes from the Holy Table when all things are pre-

pared, either does not understand his duty, or does not care for the dying command of his Saviour, the forgiveness of his sins, the strengthening of his soul, and the refreshing it with the hope of glory.

"With the first Christians the Christian Sacrifice was a constant part of the Lord's-day service. For several centuries they received the blessed Sacrament every day, and their opinion of those who turned their back upon it may be gathered from the ancient canon, ' If any believer join in the prayers of the faithful, and go away without receiving the Lord's Supper, let him be excommunicate, as bringing confusion into the Church of God.'

"We have no right to reject God's commands, or to choose between them. Considering this, therefore, to be a command of God, he that does not communicate as often as he can has no piety; considering it as a mercy, he that does not communicate as often as he can has no wisdom."

To the objection of some persons, that they cannot communicate often, because they cannot pretend to lead so holy a life as constantly communicating would oblige them to do, Wesley answers: " This would be an argument against communicating at all; for if they cannot live up to the profession of those who communicate once a week, neither can they live up to the profession of those who communicate once a year. But if this be true, it would be better for them that they had never been born. To say this is neither better nor worse than renouncing Christianity. It is in effect renouncing their baptism, wherein

they solemnly promised to keep all God's command-
ments."

The way in which Wesley answers another objection deserves notice. It is the very common one,
"I have communicated constantly so long, but I
have not found the benefit I expected." Here is
the answer: "This has been the case with many
well-meaning persons, and therefore deserves to be
particularly considered. And consider this first:
whatever God commands us to do, we are to do,
because He commands, whether we feel any benefit
thereby or no. Now God commands, 'Do this in
remembrance of Me.' This, therefore, we are to do,
because He commands; whether we find present
benefit thereby, or not. But undoubtedly we shall
find benefit sooner or later, though perhaps insensibly.
We shall be insensibly strengthened, made more fit
for the service of God, and more constant in it."[1]

2. Second, as to the Daily Sacrifice. Wesley con-.
sistently taught that this was the ancient practice,
and that a restoration of this privilege was much to
be desired. Hence in his "Sixth Discourse upon the
Sermon on the Mount," commenting on the words,
"Give us this day our daily bread," he remarks:
"We understand, not barely the outward bread, . . .
but much more the spiritual bread, the grace of God,
the food 'which endureth unto everlasting life.' It
was the judgment of many of the ancient Fathers,
that we are here to understand the Sacramental
Bread also, daily received in the beginning by the

[1] Sermon cvi.

whole Church of Christ, and highly esteemed till the love of many waxed cold, as the grand channel whereby the grace of His Spirit was conveyed to the souls of all the children of God."[1]   This necessary and beneficial truth Wesley sought to impress upon all his followers ; for in his instructions to Christians he asks and answers, "How often did the first Christians receive the Lord's Supper ?   Every day; it was their daily bread."   And again, in the sermon on the "Duty of Constant Communion," from which we have before quoted: "With the first Christians the Christian Sacrifice was a constant part of the Lord's-day service.   And for several centuries they received it almost every day; four times a week always, and every Saint's day beside."[2]   He urged also upon his own people the very evident fact that the judgment of our own Church is quite in favour of constant communion, and that she has taken " all possible care that the Sacrament be duly administered whenever the Common Prayer is read, every Sunday and Holiday in the year."[3]

Besides this, whenever and wherever practicable, Wesley showed by his own practice the value he set upon a Daily Celebration of the Holy Communion, and his journals abound with expressions like the following :—

1737. "Sunday, April 3rd, and every day in this great and holy week, we had a sermon and the Holy Communion."[4]

---

[1] Sermon xxvi.   [2] Sermon cvi.   [3] Sermon cvi.
[4] Journal, vol. i., p. 44.

1774. "December 25th. During the twelve festival days we had the Lord's Supper daily: a little emblem of the Primitive Church. May we be followers of them in all things, as they were of Christ."[1]

1777. "Easter day was a solemn and comfortable day wherein God was remarkably present with His people. During the Octave I administered the Lord's Supper every morning, after the example of the Primitive Church."[2]

3. Third, as to the principle of the outward commemorative Sacrifice, what can be more explicit than the following extracts? The first is from a letter to Wesley's Brother-in-law, Mr. Hall, in answer to some strictures that the latter had written upon his conduct. "We believe there is, and always was, in every Christian Church (whether dependent upon the Bishop of Rome or not), an outward priesthood ordained by Jesus Christ, and an *outward Sacrifice* offered therein, by men authorized to act as ambassadors of Christ, and stewards of the Mysteries of God."[3] This is as distinct a recognition of the Priesthood and the Sacrifice as could possibly be expressed in words.

My second extract is from the "Notes on the New Testament," a work recognized as official, even by the Wesleyan Conference of the present day. "'Do this in remembrance of Me.' The ancient sacrifices were in remembrance of sin. This Sacrifice, once

---

[1] Journal, vol. iv., p. 37.   [2] Journal, vol. iv., p. 90.
[3] Journal, vol. ii., p. 4.

offered, is *still represented* in remembrance of the remission of sins.[1]"

The following extract on the subject of Eucharistic Adoration is from Wesley's reply to a Roman Catechism, a pamphlet written for the express purpose of guarding his followers against mistaken notions. "We freely own that Christ is to be adored in the Lord's Supper; but that the elements are to be adored we deny."[2] This latter is a distinction familiar to most Catholic Churchmen, but lest it might be misunderstood I will give a similar quotation from a memorial, presented to the Archbishop of Canterbury, which was signed by most of the leading Anglo-Catholic clergy :—

"We repudiate all 'adoration' of the Sacramental Bread and Wine, which would be 'idolatry;' regarding them with the reverence due to them, because of their Sacramental relation to the Body and Blood of our Lord : we repudiate, also, all adoration of a 'Corporal Presence of CHRIST's Natural Flesh and Blood'—that is to say, of the Presence of His Body and Blood as they 'are in heaven.'

"We believe that Christ Himself, really and truly, but spiritually and ineffably, present in the Sacrament, is *therein* to be adored."

IV. There are two other matters in connection with the Holy Eucharist, only slightly referred to in the "Hymns on the Lord's Supper." Nevertheless, as they are of some little importance, because they

[1] Wesley's Works, vol. xv., p. 259.
[2] Wesley's Works, vol. x., p. 117.

serve to identify Wesley as the harbinger of the Catholic revival in the Church of England, I purpose to give his deliberate opinion about them. They are, first, The mingling of water with the Wine used in Holy Communion, referred to in the following lines:—

> " See from His wounded side,
> The *mingled* current flow !
> The WATER and the BLOOD applied,
> Shall wash us white as snow."   *Hymn* lxxiv.

Second, the practice of chorally celebrating the Holy Communion, which seems to me to be clearly implied in the hymn where Wesley invokes angels to join in the song wherewith we greet the Presence of the Son of God upon our Altars:—

> " Ye that round our Altars throng.
> Listening Angels, join the song;
> Sing with us, ye heavenly powers;
> Pardon, grace, and glory ours."   *Hymn* clxiv.

As to the first. In a manuscript still in existence, and supposed to be written in the year 1741, Wesley, in his own handwriting, penned the following words: " I believe it (myself) a *duty* to observe, so far as I can, to use WATER in the Eucharist."[1] He transcribed also, for the use of Methodists, the " Apology " of Justin Martyr, containing the following account: " Prayers being over, bread, and a cup of *wine* and *water* are brought to the Bishop, which he takes,

---

[1] " John Wesley's Place in Church History," p. 69.

and offers up praise and glory to the Father of all things, through the name of His Son and Holy Spirit. The people answer, with joyful acclamations, Amen! then the consecrated elements, the Eucharistical Bread and Wine, are distributed to, and partaken by, all that are present. . . . We do not take this as common bread and common wine, but as the Flesh and Blood of the Incarnate Jesus."[1] And yet again, in a controversy with the Rev. Dr. Middleton, Wesley enforces and defends the practice in the following words: " You say, 'In the Sacrament of the Eucharist several abuses were introduced.' You instance, first, in mixing the wine with the water. But how does it appear that this was any abuse at all? or, that 'Irenæus declared it to have been taught as well as practised by our Saviour?' The words you quote to prove this do not prove it at all; they simply relate a matter of fact: ' Taking the Bread, He confessed it to be His Body, and the Mixed Cup He affirmed it was His Blood.' You cannot be ignorant of this fact, that the cup used after the Paschal Supper was always mixed with water."[2]

As to the second; namely, choral celebration of the Holy Communion. In an age of peculiar spiritual deadness, when all earnest work seemed to have died away; when the worship of God was conducted in the most disgraceful and slovenly manner, and the Holy Communion was scarcely ever celebrated;

---

[1] Wesley's Works. Pine ed., Bristol, 1773, vol. ix., pp. 27, 28.

[2] Wesley's Works, vol. x., p. 8.

Wesley wrote hymns for his associates to sing during and after the Sacrament;[1] and in his Journal many times expressed his approval, when the highest triumphs of musical art were used to adorn the Holy Sacrifice, and glorify the Sacramental Presence of Christ. Of such a nature are the following extracts :—

1762. "Sunday. At the Cathedral . . . the whole service was performed with great seriousness and decency. Such an organ I never saw or heard before, so large, beautiful, and so finely toned. And the music of ' Glory be to God in the Highest,' I think, exceeded the ' Messiah' itself."[2]

1782. "Sunday. I was much pleased with the decent behaviour of the whole congregation at the Cathedral, as also with the solemn music at the post-Communion, one of the finest compositions I ever heard."[3]

1782. "I came to assist Mr. Simpson. While we were administering the Sacrament, I heard a low, soft, solemn sound, just like that of an Æolian harp. It continued five or six minutes, and so affected many that they could not refrain from tears. It then gradually died away. Strange that no other organist (that I know) should think of this."[4]

---

[1] In reading the hymns this fact should always be borne in mind, because, when the hymns are diverted from their original purpose, it is easy to assign to many of the expressions an entirely different meaning.

[2] Journal, vol. iii., p. 106.   [3] Journal, vol. iv., p. 222.

[4] Journal, vol. iv., p. 212.

Thus Wesley records his sympathy with a movement which, in these days, is looked upon with so much suspicion. Had he lived in our time, there can be no reasonable doubt that he would have been, if not in the vanguard of the Catholic movement, at least an earnest worker for the restoration of all Catholic privileges. To prove this, I might go on quoting extracts from Wesley's writings to an almost indefinite extent; but my purpose is accomplished, and so I leave the matter in the hands of my readers. If any care to pursue the subject further, let me recommend them to read a work by the Rev. H. W. Holden, called "John Wesley in company with High Churchmen." The parallel it works out is complete, and the book is written in a spirit of charity and love which might with advantage be copied by all controversial writers.

Two objections, very often urged by Wesleyan controversialists, it may be as well to notice before concluding. First, it is constantly said that, although Wesley was an extreme High Churchman during the early part of his life, after his conversion he gradually relinquished all these notions. In reply to this, it is only necessary to say that neither the "Altar Companion" nor the Hymns were printed until some years after his conversion, and both were reprinted many times during his subsequent life. Again, it is said: "Wesley so often speaks of the Consecrated Bread and Wine as 'Signs' or 'Tokens' of Christ's Body and Blood, that he could not have believed that Christ Himself was really present in the Sacrament." To those who carefully read the hymns I need not point out that Wesley speaks so explicitly as to the doctrine of the Real Presence, that there can be no misapprehension of his meaning. But to those who are disposed to raise a quibble, I answer, "The use of the words 'Signs' or 'Tokens,' although at first sight open to misconception by those persons who do not understand the doctrine of the Holy Eucharist, is correct in the strict theological sense of the terms." It is not my design here to enter into the discussion of these questions; but I may simply remark, that if Wesley erred in this respect, he erred in the very best company. St. Thomas Aquinas, the great Eucharistic poet of the Catholic Church, uses similar language in a hymn, now sung as a sequence by the Roman Church, on the festival of Corpus Christi, a day specially set apart for the joyful commemoration of this great and holy Mystery.

> " Sub diversis speciébus
> Signis tantum, et non rebus
>   Latent res eximiœ
> Caro cibus, sanguis potus;
> Manem tamen Christus totus
>   Sub utráque spécie."

The verse is thus paraphrased in the " Hymnal Noted."

> " Here beneath these *signs* are hidden
> Priceless things to sense forbidden;
>   *Signs*, not things, are all we see:
> Blood is pour'd, and Flesh is broken,
> Yet in either wondrous *Token*,
>   CHRIST Entire we know to be."

So even the Roman Church by adopting this language has sanctioned its use, and if St. Thomas Aquinas found it compatible with belief in the doctrine of the Real Presence, and Wesley expresses his belief in the same doctrine in words whose import cannot be mistaken, surely it will not be denied that Wesley used the words in the same sense as they were used by the great theologian and poet.

It is in the hope that some who call themselves by Wesley's name may be induced to follow Wesley's example and teaching, that I have ventured to re-publish this once popular, but now neglected and almost forgotten book. To Methodists it will be useful, as showing the real opinions of him whom they call their founder upon one of the most important questions that now agitate and disturb the religious world. If they will read and study it carefully, they will doubtless rise from its perusal with higher and more exalted views of that profound Mystery by which we are sensibly united to God.

To Churchmen it will be useful as a handbook of Sacramental teaching, compiled by a Priest of their own Communion, whose name now commands almost as much reverence as it once suffered obloquy for the cause of Catholic truth. It will also serve them as a book of devotions and meditations for use during the Celebration of the Holy Eucharist. May I ask all Churchmen who thus use it to pray that the purpose of the publication may be answered, and that God in His own good time may again unite Churchmen and Dissenters in a bond of holy union, for the defence of the Catholic Faith and for the glory of His own Holy Name?

"That they all may be one, as Thou, Father, art in Me, and I in Thee ; that they also may be one in Us ; that the world may believe that Thou hast sent Me." (John xvii. 21.)

W. E. D.

A

COMPANION

FOR THE

ALTAR.

Extracted from THOMAS à KEMPIS.

BY

JOHN WESLEY, M.A.

FELLOW OF LINCOLN COLLEGE, OXFORD.

THE FOURTH EDITION.

LONDON:

PRINTED IN THE YEAR MDCCXLVIII.

Fac-simile.

A

Companion for the Altar.

AN EXHORTATION

UNTO THE HOLY COMMUNION.

THE VOICE OF CHRIST.

COME unto Me, all ye that travail and are heavy laden, and I will refresh you.

The Bread which I give is my Flesh, which I give for the Life of the World.

Take, eat, This is my Body which is given for you: do this in Remembrance of Me.

He that eateth my Flesh, and drinketh my Blood, dwelleth in Me, and I in him.

The Words which I speak unto you are Spirit and Life.

CHAPTER I.

With how great reverence CHRIST ought to be received.

THE VOICE OF THE DISCIPLE.

1.

THESE are Thy Words, O CHRIST, the everlasting Truth.

Because therefore they are Thine and true, they are all thankfully to be received by me.

They are Thine, and Thou hast spoken them; and they are mine also, because Thou hast spoken them for my salvation.

I willingly receive them from Thy mouth, that they may be the deeper imprinted in my heart.

These gracious Words, so full of sweetness and love, encourage me; but my own offences drive me back from receiving so great Mysteries.

2. Thou commandest me to come confidently unto Thee, if I will have part with Thee; to receive the Food of Immortality, if I desire to obtain everlasting glory.

Come, sayest Thou, *unto Me, all ye that travail and are heavy laden, and I will refresh you.*

O sweet and friendly word in the ear of sinners, that Thou, my LORD GOD, should invite the poor and needy to the partaking of Thy most Holy Body!

But who am I, LORD, that I should presume to approach unto Thee?

Behold, the Heaven of Heavens cannot contain Thee, and Thou sayest, *Come ye* ALL *unto Me.*

3. What meaneth this so gracious condescension, this so friendly invitation?

How shall I dare to come, that know no good in myself?

How shall I bring Thee into my house, that have so often offended Thy most gracious countenance?

The Angels and Archangels revere Thee, the saints and just men fear Thee, and Thou sayest, *Come ye all unto Me!*

Unless Thou, O LORD, didst say it, who would believe it to be true?

And unless Thou didst command it, who would dare to come unto Thee?

Behold, *Noah*, a just man, laboured a hundred years in the making of the Ark, that he might be saved with a few; and how can I in one hour prepare myself to receive with reverence the Maker of the world?

4. *Moses*, Thy great servant, and Thy special friend, made an Ark of incorruptible wood, which also he covered with most pure gold, to put the

tables of the Law therein ; and I, a corruptible creature, how shall I dare so lightly to receive the Maker of the Law, and the Giver of life ?

Solomon, the wisest of the Kings of *Israel,* bestowed seven years in building a magnificent Temple to the praise of Thy Name.

He celebrated the Feast of the Dedication thereof eight days together : he offered a thousand peace-offerings, and he solemnly set the Ark in the place prepared for it, with the sound of trumpets, and joy.

And, I the most miserable and poorest of men, how shall I bring Thee into my house, that can scarce spend one half-hour devoutly ? Yea, would I could once spend near an half-hour in due manner !

5. O my GOD, how much did they do out of an endeavour to please Thee !

And, alas ! how little is that which I do ! I am very seldom wholly recollected, very seldom free from distraction.

And yet surely no unbecoming thought ought to appear in the Presence of Thy Deity, nor any creature find any place in me ; for I am not to harbour an Angel, but the LORD of Angels.

Why therefore am I not more inflamed at Thy venerable Presence ?

6. The most devout King *David* danced before the Ark of GOD with all his might, calling to mind the benefits bestowed in times past upon his forefathers.

C

He made instruments of sundry kinds; he composed Psalms, and appointed them to be sung with joy.

He also often sung himself to the harp, being inspired with the HOLY GHOST.

He taught the people of *Israel* to bless GOD with their whole heart, and with joint voices every day to bless and praise Him.

If so great devotion was then shewn, and there was such celebrating of the Divine praise before the Ark of the Covenant; with what reverence and devotion ought I to receive the most precious Body and Blood of CHRIST?

7. O GOD, the invisible Creator of the world, how wonderfully dost Thou deal with us!

How sweetly and graciously dost Thou dispose of all things with those to whom Thou offerest Thyself in this Holy Sacrament!

This exceedeth all understanding! This strongly draweth the hearts of the devout, and inflameth their affections.

8. O the admirable and hidden Grace of this Sacrament, which such as will be slaves unto sin cannot experience!

In this Sacrament spiritual grace is given, the strength which was lost is restored in the soul, and the beauty disfigured by sin returneth again.

This Grace is sometimes so great that not only the mind, but the weak body also, feeleth great increase of strength.

9. Our coldness and negligence is much to be

bewailed, that we are not drawn with greater affection to receive CHRIST, in Whom all the hope and merit of those that are saved consists.

For He is our sanctification and redemption; He is the comfort of us travellers, and the everlasting enjoyment of saints.

It is much, therefore, to be lamented that many so little consider this blessed Mystery, which rejoiceth Heaven, and preserveth the whole world.

O the blindness and hardness of man's heart, that doth not more deeply weigh so unspeakable a gift!

Thanks be unto Thee, gracious Jesus, the everlasting Shepherd, that hast vouchsafed to refresh us poor exiles with Thy precious Body and Blood, and to invite us to the receiving of these Mysteries with the words of Thy own mouth, saying, *Come unto Me, all ye that travail and are heavy laden, and I will refresh you.*

CHAPTER II.

That the great Goodness and Love of God *is exhibited
to Man in this Sacrament.*

THE VOICE OF THE DISCIPLE.

. 1 .

IN confidence of Thy goodness, I come, O
Lord, a sick man unto my Saviour, hungry and thirsty to the Fountain of Life,
needy to the King of Heaven, a servant
unto my Lord, a creature to my Creator, disconso-
late to Thee my merciful Comforter.

But whence is this to me, that Thou vouchsafest
to come unto me? who am I, that Thou shouldest
give Thyself unto me?

How dare a sinner appear before Thee? And
how is it that Thou dost vouchsafe to come unto a
sinner?

Thou knowest Thy servant, and seest that he hath
no good thing in him for which Thou shouldest
bestow this favour upon him.

I confess therefore my unworthiness, I acknowledge Thy goodness, I praise Thy mercy, and give Thee thanks for this Thy transcendent love.

For Thou dost this for Thine own sake, not for any merits of mine; that Thy goodness may be better known unto me, Thy love more abundantly shewed, and Thy gracious condescension the more eminently displayed.

Since, therefore, it is Thy pleasure, and Thou hast commanded that it should be so, this Thy favour is also pleasing to me, and may my sins be no hindrance.

2. O most gracious JESUS, how great reverence and thanks, together with perpetual praise, are due unto Thee for the receiving of Thy sacred Body, whose preciousness no man is able to express!

But what shall I think of, now that I am to approach unto my LORD, whom I am not able duly to honour, and yet I desire to receive Him with devotion?

What is better than to humble myself wholly before Thee, and to exalt Thy infinite goodness over me?

I praise Thee, my GOD, and will exalt Thee for ever: I despise and submit myself unto Thee, in a deep sense of my own unworthiness.

3. Behold, Thou art the Holy of Holies, and I the vilest of sinners!

Behold, Thou inclinest unto me, who am not worthy so much as to look up unto Thee!

Behold, Thou comest unto me, it is Thy will to be with me, Thou invitest me to Thy Banquet.

Thou wilt give me the Food of Heaven, the Bread of Angels, to eat; which is no other than Thyself the Living Bread that descended from Heaven, and giveth Life unto the world.

4. Behold from whence doth this love proceed! what a gracious condescension appeareth herein! how great thanks and praises are due unto Thee for these benefits!

O how good wast Thou when Thou ordainedst it! How sweet and pleasant the Banquet, when Thou gavest Thyself to be our Food!

How wonderful is Thy operation, O LORD! how mighty is Thy power! how unspeakable is Thy truth!

For Thou hast said the word, and all things were made; and this was done which Thou commandedst.

5. A thing of great admiration, that Thou, my LORD GOD, shouldest be exhibited unto us by the elements of Bread and Wine.

Thou, who art the LORD of all things, and standest in need of none, hast pleased to dwell in us by means of this Thy Sacrament.

Preserve my heart and body undefiled, that with a cheerful and pure conscience I may always celebrate Thy Mysteries, and receive them to my everlasting health: which Thou hast ordained for Thy honour and for a perpetual memorial.

6. Rejoice, O my soul, and give thanks unto GOD, for so excellent a gift, so singular a comfort left unto me in this vale of tears.

For as often as thou celebratest this Mystery, and receivest the Body of CHRIST, so often art thou made partaker of all the merits of CHRIST.

For the love of CHRIST is never diminished, and the greatness of His propitiation is never exhausted :

Therefore thou oughtest always to weigh with attentive consideration this great Mystery of Thy salvation.

So great, new, and joyful it ought to seem unto Thee when thou comest to these holy Mysteries ; as if the same day CHRIST first descending into the Womb of the Virgin was become man ; or, hanging on the Cross, did suffer and die for the salvation of mankind.

CHAPTER III.

That it is profitable to communicate often.

THE VOICE OF THE DISCIPLE.

1.

BEHOLD, O Lord, I come unto Thee, that I may be comforted by Thy gift, and delighted in Thy holy Banquet, which Thou, O God, hast prepared in Thy goodness for the poor.

Behold, in Thee is all that I can or ought to desire : Thou art my Salvation and my Redemption, my Hope and my Strength, my Honour and my Glory.

Make joyful therefore this day the soul of Thy servant ; for I have lifted it up unto Thee, O Lord Jesus.

I desire to receive Thee now with devotion and reverence. I long to bring Thee into my house, that with *Zaccheus* I may be blessed by Thee, and numbered amongst the children of *Abraham*.

My soul thirsteth to receive Thy Body and Blood, my heart desireth to be united with Thee.

2. Give me Thyself, and it sufficeth: but without Thee no comfort is available.

I cannot be without Thee, nor live without Thy visitation:

And therefore I must often come unto Thee, and receive Thee for the welfare of my soul; lest haply I faint by the way if I be deprived of the heavenly Food.

For so, most merciful Jesus, Thou once didst say, preaching to the people, and curing sundry diseases, I will not send them home fasting, lest they faint by the way.

Deal Thou therefore in like manner now with me, who hast vouchsafed to leave Thyself in this Sacrament for the comfort of the faithful.

For Thou art the sweet refreshment of the soul; and he that eateth Thee worthily shall be a partaker of everlasting glory.

3. O the wonderful condescension of Thy mercy towards us, that Thou, O Lord God, the Creator and Giver of life to all spirits, dost vouchsafe to come unto a poor soul, and with Thy whole Deity to replenish her hunger!

O happy mind and blessed soul that receives Thee, her Lord God, with devout affection, and in receiving of Thee is filled with spiritual joy!

O how great a Lord doth she entertain! How beloved a Guest doth she harbour! How pleasant a Companion doth she receive! How faithful a Friend doth she take in! How lovely and glorious a Spouse doth she embrace!

She embraceth Him who is to be loved above all that is beloved, and above all things that may be desired.

Let heaven and earth, and all the hosts of them, be silent in Thy Presence: for what praise and beauty soever they have, it is received from Thy bounty, and cannot equal the beauty of Thy Name, of whose wisdom there is no number.

CHAPTER IV.

That many Gifts are bestowed upon them that communicate devoutly.

THE VOICE OF THE DISCIPLE.

1.

Y LORD GOD, prevent Thy servant with the blessings of Thy goodness, that I may approach devoutly to Thy glorious Sacrament:

Stir up my heart unto Thee, and deliver me from a heavy numbness of mind.

Visit me with Thy salvation, that I may taste in spirit Thy sweetness, which plentifully lieth in this Sacrament, as a fountain.

Enlighten also my eyes to behold so great a Mystery, and strengthen me to believe it with steady faith.

For it is Thy work, and not man's power; Thy sacred institution, not man's invention.

For no man is of himself able to comprehend these things, which surpass the understanding of Angels.

What therefore shall I, unworthy sinner, dust and ashes, be able to comprehend of so high and sacred a Mystery!

2. O Lord, in the simplicity of my heart, at Thy commandment I come unto Thee with hope and reverence, and do truly believe that Thou art present in this Sacrament.

Thy will is that I receive Thee, and that by love I unite myself unto Thee.

Wherefore I implore Thy mercy, and crave Thy special grace, that I may wholly melt, and overflow with love unto Thee; and hereafter never seek any comfort out of Thee.

For this most high and worthy Sacrament is the health of the soul and body, the remedy of all spiritual weakness; hereby my vices are cured, my passions bridled, temptations overcome, grace infused, holiness increased, faith confirmed, hope strengthened, and love inflamed.

3. For Thou hast bestowed, and still dost bestow, many benefits in this Sacrament upon Thy children; O my God, the Protector of my soul, the Repairer of human weakness, and the Giver of all inward comfort;

Thou impartest unto them much comfort against sundry tribulations;

Thou liftest them up from the depth of their own misery, to hope in Thy protection.

Who is there, that approaching humbly unto the Fountain of Sweetness, doth not carry away from thence at least some little sweetness?

.Or who, standing by a great fire, receiveth not some small heat thereby?

And Thou art a Fountain always full and over-flowing, a Fire ever burning, and never decaying.

4. Wherefore, if I cannot draw out of the full Fountain itself, nor drink my fill, I will notwithstanding set my lips to the mouth of this heavenly Conduit, that I may draw from thence at least some small drop to refresh my thirst, and not wholly be dried up.

And though I be not so inflamed as the Cherubim and Seraphim; notwithstanding I will endeavour after some small spark of Divine fire, by humbly receiving of this enlivening Sacrament.

And whatsoever is wanting in me, O merciful JESUS, do Thou graciously supply, who hast vouch-safed to call ALL unto Thee, saying, *Come unto Me, all ye that travail and are heavy laden, and I will refresh you.*

5. I indeed labour in the sweat of my brow, I am vexed with grief of heart, I am burthened with sin, I am troubled with temptations, I am entangled with many evil passions; and there is none to help me, none to deliver me, but Thou, O LORD, my SAVIOUR, to whom I commit myself and all that is mine, that Thou mayest keep me to life everlasting.

CHAPTER V.

*Of the examining our conscience and giving up
ourselves to God.*

1.

ABOVE all things, thou oughtest to receive this Sacrament with great humility of heart, and lowly reverence.

And, if thou hast time, confess unto God in the secret of thine heart all the miseries of thy disordered passions.

2. Lament and grieve, that thou art yet so carnal, so worldly, so unmortified as to thy passions;

So unwatchful over thy outward senses, so often entangled with vain imaginations;

So negligent and cold in prayer, so undevout in celebrating, so dry in receiving;

So quickly distracted, so seldom wholly recollected;

So suddenly moved to anger, so apt to take displeasure against another; and speak evil of others;

So prone to judge;

So often purposing much good, and yet performing little.

3. These and other thy defects being confessed, with full resignation, and with thy whole will, offer up thyself a perpetual sacrifice to the honour of My Name on the altar of thy heart, faithfully committing thy body and soul unto Me;

That so thou mayest receive profitably the Sacrament of My Body.

4. For a man hath no other oblation, than to offer up himself unto GOD in the Holy Communion.

And whensoever he shall come to Me for pardon and grace, as I live, saith the LORD, who will not the death of a sinner, but rather that he be converted and live, I will not remember his sins any more, but they shall be all forgiven him.

5. As I willingly offered up Myself unto GOD My Father for thy sins, My hands being stretched forth on the Cross, and My Body naked, so that nothing remained in me that was not wholly turned into a Sacrifice, for the appeasing the Divine Majesty:

So oughtest thou also to offer up thyself willingly unto Me every day, as a pure and holy oblation, with all thy might and affections, in as hearty a manner as thou canst.

What do I require of thee more than that thou entirely resign thyself unto Me?

Whatsoever thou givest besides thyself is of no account in My sight; for I seek not thy gifts, but thyself.

6. As it would not suffice thee to have all things

besides Me ; so neither can it please Me, whatsoever thou givest, if thou offerest not thyself.

Offer up thyself unto Me, and give thyself wholly to God, and thy offering shall be accepted.

Behold, I offered up Myself wholly unto My Father for thee, that I might be wholly thine, and thou remain Mine.

But if thou abidest in thyself, and dost not offer thyself up freely unto My will, thy oblation is not entire, neither will the union between us be perfect.

Therefore, a free offering up of thyself into the hands of God ought to go before all thy actions, if thou wilt obtain freedom and grace.

For this cause so few become INWARDLY free, because they cannot wholly deny themselves.

My saying is unalterable, *Unless a man forsake all, he cannot be My disciple.*

Therefore if thou desirest to be My disciple, offer up thyself unto Me with thy whole affections.

CHAPTER VI.

That we ought to offer up ourselves and all that is ours, unto God, and to pray for all.

THE VOICE OF THE DISCIPLE.

1.

THINE, O Lord, are all things that are in heaven and in earth.

I desire to offer up myself unto Thee, as a free oblation, and to remain always Thine.

O Lord, in the simplicity of my heart I offer myself unto Thee this day, for a sacrifice of perpetual praise, to be Thy servant for ever.

2. I offer unto Thee, O Lord, all my sins and offences, which I have committed before Thee and Thy holy angels, from the day wherein I first could sin to this hour, upon Thy merciful Altar.

Consume and burn them all with the fire of Thy love, and wash out all the stains of my sins.

O cleanse my conscience from all offences, and restore to me again Thy grace, which I lost by sin, fully forgiving me all my offences, and receiving me mercifully with a kiss of peace.

3. What can I do for my sins, but humbly confess and bewail them, and incessantly entreat Thy favour ?

I beseech Thee, hear me graciously when I stand before Thee, O my GOD !

All my sins are very displeasing unto me. I will never commit them any more ; but I bewail them, and am purposed to repent, and according to the utmost of my power to please Thee.

Forgive me, O GOD, forgive me my sins, for Thy holy Name's sake.

Save my soul, which Thou hast redeemed with Thy most precious Blood.

Behold, I commit myself to Thy mercy, I resign myself into Thy hands.

Do with me according to Thy goodness, not according to my wickedness and iniquity.

4. I offer up also unto Thee all whatsoever good Thou hast given me, although it be very little and imperfect, that Thou mayest amend and sanctify it ;

That Thou mayest make it grateful and acceptable unto Thee, and always perfect it more and more ;

And bring me also, who am a slothful and unprofitable creature, to a good and blessed end.

5. I offer up also unto Thee all the pious desires of devout persons, the necessities of my parents, friends, brethren, sisters, and of all those that are dear unto me, and that have done good, either to myself or to others, for Thy love.

And that have desired me to pray for them and all

theirs: that they all may receive the help of Thy grace and comfort, protection from danger, deliverance from pain; and, being freed from all evils, may joyfully give worthy thanks unto Thee.

6. I offer up also unto Thee my prayers especially for them who have in anything wronged, or grieved, or slandered me, or have done me any damage or displeasure;

And for all those also whom I have at any time troubled, grieved, or scandalized, by words or deeds, wittingly, or unawares; that it may please Thee to forgive us all our sins and offences one against another.

Take, O Lord, from our hearts all jealousy, indignation, wrath, and contention, and whatsoever may impair charity and lessen brotherly love.

Have mercy, O Lord, have mercy on those that crave Thy mercy: give grace unto them that stand in need thereof: and grant that we may be counted worthy to enjoy Thy grace, and to attain to life everlasting.   Amen.

CHAPTER VII.

That the BODY *of* CHRIST, *and the Holy Scripture, are most necessary unto a faithful soul.*

THE VOICE OF THE DISCIPLE.

1.

O LORD JESUS, how great sweetness hath a soul that feasteth with Thee in Thy Banquet, where there is set no other food but Thyself, her only Beloved, and most to be desired above all the desires of her heart!

And verily it would be a sweet thing unto me to pour out tears from the very bottom of my heart in Thy presence: and with holy *Magdalene* to wash Thy feet with my tears.

But where is this devotion? where is this so plentiful shedding of holy tears?

Surely in the sight of Thee and Thy holy angels my whole heart should be inflamed, and even weep for joy!

For I enjoy thee in the Sacrament, truly present, though hidden under another representation.

2. For to behold Thee in Thine own Divine brightness, mine eyes would not be able to endure it.

Neither could the whole world stand in the brightness of the glory of Thy Majesty.

I enjoy Him whom the angels adore in heaven :

But I, as yet, by faith ; they by sight, and without
a veil.

I ought to be content with the light of true faith,
and to walk therein until the day of everlasting
brightness breaks forth, and the shadows of figures
pass away.

For when that which is perfect shall come, the use
of Sacraments shall cease.

For the Blessed in Heaven need not any Sacramental remedy, but rejoice without end in the presence of GOD.

Beholding His glory face to face, and being trans-
formed from glory to glory in the image of the incomprehensible Deity, they taste the word of God
made flesh, as he was from the beginning, and as He
remaineth for ever.

3. Thou art my witness, O God, that nothing can
comfort me ; no creature can give me rest, but Thou,
O God, whom I desire to behold everlastingly.

But I submit myself to Thee in all my desires.

For Thy saints, also, O Lord, who now rejoice
with Thee, whilst they lived, expected in faith and
great patience the coming of Thy glory.   What they
believed, I believe : what they hoped for, I also hope
for : whither they are come, I trust I shall come by
Thy grace.

In the meantime I will go forward in faith,
strengthened by their examples :

I have also Thy holy Book for my comfort and guide, and Thy most holy Body for a remedy and refuge.

4. I perceive two things to be especially necessary in this life, without which it would be insupportable.

Whilst I am kept in the prison of this body I chiefly need two things, to wit, food and light.

Thou hast therefore given unto me Thy sacred Body and Blood for the nourishment of my soul; and Thou hast set Thy Word as a light unto my feet.

Without these two I could not well live.

For the Word of God is the light of the soul, and Thy Sacrament the Bread of Life.

Thanks be unto Thee, O Jesus Christ, the Light of everlasting life, for the holy doctrine which Thou hast afforded us by Thy servants the prophets and apostles.

5. Thanks be unto Thee, O Thou Creator and Redeemer of man, who, to manifest Thy love to the whole world, hast prepared a great supper, wherein Thou hast set before us to be eaten Thy most sacred Body and Blood.

Rejoicing all the faithful with Thy holy Banquet, and replenishing them with the Cup of Salvation; and the holy angels do feast with us, but yet with a more happy sweetness.

6. O how great and honourable is the office of God's ministers, to whom it is given with sacred words to consecrate the Sacrament of the Lord of

glory, with their lips to bless, with their hands to hold, with their mouth to receive, and also to administer to others.

Nothing but what is holy, no word but good and profitable, ought to proceed from his mouth who so often receiveth the Sacrament of CHRIST.

7. Assist, Almighty God, with Thy grace, that they who have undertaken the office of priesthood may serve Thee worthily and devoutly in all purity.

And if they have not lived in so great innocency as they ought, grant them at least duly to bewail their sins which they have committed, and in the spirit of humility, with full purpose of heart, to serve Thee hereafter more fervently.

CHAPTER VIII.

How he who is to communicate ought to prepare himself.

THE VOICE OF THE BELOVED.

1.

 AM the Lover of purity, and the Giver of all holiness.

I seek a pure heart, and there is the place of My rest.

Make ready and adorn for Me the great chamber, and I will keep with thee the Passover among My disciples.

2. Know thou notwithstanding, that the merit of no action of thine is able to make this preparation, although thou shouldst prepare thyself a whole year together, and think of nothing else.

Thou art of My mere grace and favour suffered to come to My Table,

Like a beggar invited to dinner to a rich man, who hath nothing else to return him for his benefits but to humble himself and give him thanks.

Do what lieth in thee, and do it diligently, not for

custom, not for necessity, but with fear and reverence and affection receive thy beloved Lord God, who vouchsafeth to come unto thee.

I am He that hath called thee, I have commanded it to be done, I will supply what is wanting in thee : come and receive Me.

3. When I bestow the grace of devotion, give thanks to thy God ; for it is given thee, not for that thou art worthy, but because I have mercy on thee.

If thou hast it not, but dost feel thyself dry ; continue in prayer, sigh and knock, and give not over until thou receive some drop of saving grace.

Thou hast need of Me, not I of thee.

Neither comest thou to sanctify Me, but I come to sanctify and improve thee.

Thou comest that thou mayest be sanctified by Me, and united unto Me, that thou mayest receive new grace, and be inflamed anew to amendment.

CHAPTER IX.

That we ought to desire with our whole heart to be united to CHRIST *in the Sacrament.*

1.

HO will give me, O LORD, to find Thee alone, and to open my whole heart unto Thee, and enjoy Thee as my soul desireth ?

And that no creature may move or regard me, but Thou alone mayest speak unto me, and I unto Thee, as the beloved is wont to speak to his beloved, and a friend to banquet with a friend.

This I pray for, this I desire, that I may be wholly united unto Thee, and may withdraw my heart from all created things.

That I may, by often communicating, learn more and more to relish heavenly and eternal things.

Ah, LORD GOD, when shall I be wholly united to Thee, and swallowed up in Thee, and altogether forgetful of myself?

Thou in me, and I in Thee, and so grant us both to continue in one.

2. Verily, Thou art my beloved, the choicest among thousands, in whom my soul is well pleased to dwell all the days of her life.

Verily, Thou art my Peacemaker, in whom is great peace and true rest, without whom is labour and sorrow and infinite misery.

Verily, Thou art a GOD that hidest Thyself, and Thy counsel is not with the wicked, but Thy speech is with the humble and simple of heart.

O LORD, how good is Thy Spirit, who to shew Thy sweetness towards Thy children, vouchsafest to feed them with the Bread of Heaven!

Verily, there is no other nation so great, that hath GOD so nigh unto them, as Thou our GOD art to all Thy faithful ones;

Unto whom, for the raising up their hearts to Heaven, Thou givest Thyself to be eaten and en-joyed.

3. For what other nation is there so honoured as the Christian people?

Or what creature under Heaven so beloved as the believing soul, whom GOD Himself feedeth with His Glorious Flesh?

O unspeakable grace! O admirable condescension! O infinite love singularly bestowed upon man!

But what shall I give unto the LORD in return for His grace, for so eminent an expression of love?

There is nothing more acceptable than to give my heart wholly to my GOD, and to unite it closely unto Him.

Then shall my inward parts rejoice, when my soul shall be perfectly united unto God.

Then He will say unto me: If thou wilt be with Me, I will be with Thee.

And I will answer Him: Vouchsafe, O Lord, to remain with me, and I will gladly be with Thee.

This is my whole desire, that my heart be united unto Thee.

4. O how great is Thy goodness, O Lord, which Thou hast laid up for them that fear Thee!

When I remember some who come with the greatest devotion and affection, I am confounded, and blush within myself that I come so heavily and coldly to Thy Table:

That I remain so dry, and without hearty affection; that I am not inflamed in Thy presence; while others, out of a vehement desire, and feeling affection of heart, cannot contain themselves from weeping.

With desire, both of soul and body, they earnestly longed after Thee, O God, the living Fountain!

Be merciful unto me, good Jesus, sweet and gracious Lord, and grant me, Thy poor needy creature, to feel sometimes, at least, in this Holy Communion, somewhat of Thy tender, cordial affection.

That my faith may be more strengthened, my hope in Thy goodness increased, and that my love once perfectly inflamed, after the tasting of the heavenly Manna, may never decay.

5. Thy mercy, O Lord, is able to give me the

grace I desire, and to visit me with the spirit of fervour when it shall please Thee.

For though I burn not with so great desire as those : yet by Thy grace I pant for this inflamed desire.

Praying and craving that I may partake with all such Thy fervent lovers, and be numbered among them.

CHAPTER X.

How the Grace of Devotion is obtained.

THE VOICE OF THE BELOVED.

1.

THOU oughtest to seek the grace of devotion fervently, to ask it earnestly, expect it patiently, and with confidence, to receive it gratefully, to keep it humbly, to work with it diligently, and to commit the time and manner of this heavenly visitation to GOD, until it please Him to come unto thee.

Thou oughtest to humble thyself when thou feelest little or no devotion ; and yet not to be too much dejected, nor to grieve inordinately.

GOD often giveth in a moment that which He hath a long time denied.

He giveth sometimes in the end that which in the beginning of prayer He deferred to grant.

It is sometimes a little thing that hindereth and hideth grace from us,

If it may be called little that hindereth so great good.

But if thou remove this, be it great or small, thou shalt have thy desire.

2. For as soon as ever thou hast delivered thyself to GOD with thy whole heart, and seekest not this or that, for thine own pleasure or will, but fixest thyself wholly upon Him, thou shalt find thyself at peace.

For nothing will then please thee so much as what pleases GOD.

3. Then shalt thou see, and be filled, and wonder, and thy heart shall be enlarged within thee, because the hand of the LORD is with thee, and He hath put Himself wholly into thy hands for ever.

Behold, so shall the man be blessed that seeketh God with his whole heart, and busieth not his soul in vain.

This man obtaineth a high degree of Divine love in receiving the Holy Eucharist.

Because he respecteth not his own devotion and comfort; but, above all devotion and comfort, the. honour and glory of GOD.

CHAPTER XI.

That we ought to lay open our necessities to Christ, *and crave His grace.*

THE VOICE OF THE DISCIPLE.

1.

O MOST loving Lord, whom I now desire to receive, Thou knowest my infirmity, and the necessity which I endure, with how many evils I am oppressed, how often I am grieved, tempted, troubled, and defiled.

I come unto Thee for remedy, I crave of Thee comfort and succour.

I speak to Him that knoweth all things, to whom all inward parts are open, and who alone can perfectly comfort and help me.

Thou knowest what good things I stand most in need of, and how poor I am in virtues.

2. Behold, I stand before Thee poor and naked, calling for grace, and craving mercy.

Refresh Thy hungry beggar, inflame my coldness with the fire of Thy love; enlighten my blindness with the brightness of Thy Presence.

Turn all earthly things to me into bitterness, all things grievous into patience, all created things into contempt and oblivion.

Lift up my heart to Thee in heaven, and suffer me not to wander upon earth.

Be Thou only sweet unto me from henceforth for evermore.

For Thou only art my meat and my drink, my love and my joy, my sweetness, and all my good.

3. O that with Thy Presence Thou wouldst wholly inflame, burn, and transform me into Thyself!

That I might be made one spirit with Thee, by the meltings of ardent love!

Suffer me not to go from Thee hungry and thirsty! but deal mercifully with me, as Thou hast often dealt wonderfully with Thy saints.

What marvel is it, if I should be wholly inflamed by Thee, and die to myself?

Since Thou art a fire always burning, and never decaying, love purifying the heart, and enlightening the understanding.

CHAPTER XII.

Of vehement desire to receive CHRIST.

THE VOICE OF THE DISCIPLE.

1.

I DESIRE to receive Thee, O LORD, with great devotion and ardent love, with the affection and fervour of my whole heart, as many saints and devout persons have desired Thee, when they received Thy Sacrament, who were most pleasing unto Thee in holiness of life, and most fervent in devotion.

O my GOD, my everlasting love, my whole good, my never-ending happiness, I would gladly receive Thee with the most vehement desire and most worthy reverence that any of the saints ever had or could feel.

2. And although I be unworthy to have all those feelings of devotion, yet I offer unto Thee the whole affection of my heart, as if I alone had all these inflamed desires:

Yea, and whatsoever an holy mind can conceive and desire, all this, with the greatest reverence and most inward affection, I offer and present unto Thee.

I desire to reserve nothing to myself, but freely and most willingly to sacrifice myself and all mine unto Thee.

My Lord God, my Creator and Redeemer: I desire to receive Thee this day with such affection, reverence, praise, and honour, with such gratitude, worthiness, and love, with such faith, hope, and purity, as Thy most holy mother, the Virgin Mary, received Thee, when she humbly answered the angel, Behold the handmaid of the Lord; let it be unto me according to thy word.

3. And as Thy blessed forerunner, *John Baptist*, leaped for joy, by reason of the Holy Ghost, whilst he was yet shut up in his mother's womb;

And afterwards seeing Jesus walking amongst men, humbling himself deeply, said with devout affection, The friend of the Bridegroom, that standeth and heareth Him, rejoiceth with joy for the voice of the Bridegroom; so I also wish to be inflamed with great and holy desires, and to offer myself up to Thee with my whole heart.

Wherefore I offer also and present unto Thee the joys, fervent affections and illuminations of all devout hearts, with all the praises celebrated by all creatures in heaven and earth, that by all Thou mayest be worthily praised and glorified for ever.

4. Receive, my Lord God, my wishes and desires of giving Thee infinite praise and immense blessing, which, according to the multitude of Thy unspeakable mercies, are most justly due unto Thee.

These I yield Thee, and desire to yield Thee every

day and moment : I do entreat and invite all heavenly minds, and all Thy devout servants, to give thanks and praises together with me.

5. Let all people, tribes, and tongues praise Thee, and magnify Thy holy Name, with the highest joy and most fervent devotion.

And let all that reverently celebrate Thy most high Sacrament, find grace and mercy at Thy hands, and pray humbly for me a sinful creature.

And when they shall have obtained their desired devotion and joyful union, and depart from Thy heavenly Table, well comforted, and marvellously refreshed, let them vouchsafe to remember my poor soul.

HYMNS

ON

THE LORD'S SUPPER.

H Y M N S

ON THE

LORD'S SUPPER.

BY

J O H N and *C H A R L E S W E S L E Y,*

Preſbyters of the Church of ENGLAND.

With a PREFACE concerning

The CHRISTIAN SACRAMENT

and SACRIFICE.

Extracted from Dr. *BREVINT.*

This do in Remembrance of Me. 1 Cor. xi. 24.

The FOURTH EDITION.

LONDON:

Printed, and ſold at the *Foundery,* MDCCLVII.

(*Fac-ſimile of original title-page.*)

The Christian Sacrament

AND SACRIFICE.

EXTRACTED FROM DR. BREVINT.

SECTION I.

The importance of well understanding the nature of this Sacrament.

1.

THE Sacrament ordained by CHRIST the night before He suffered, which St. *Paul* calls THE LORD'S SUPPER, is without doubt one of the greatest mysteries of godliness, and the most solemn feast of the Christian religion. At the holy Table the people meet to worship GOD, and GOD is present to meet and bless His people. Here we are in a special manner invited to offer up to GOD our souls, our bodies, and whatever we can *give*: and GOD offers to us the Body and Blood of His SON, and all the other blessings which we have need to *receive.* So that the holy Sacrament, like the ancient Passover, is a great mystery, consisting both of *Sacrament* and *Sacrifice;* that is, of the religious *service* which the people owe to God, and of the full *salvation* which God hath promised to His people.

2. How careful then should every Christian be to understand what so nearly concerns both his happiness and his duty! It was on this account that the devil, from the very beginning, has been so busy about this Sacrament, driving men either to make it a *false God,* or an *empty ceremony.* So much the more, let all who have either piety towards God, or any care of their own souls, so manage their devotions as to avoid superstition on the one hand, and profaneness on the other.

SECTION II.

Concerning the Sacrament, as it is a memorial of the sufferings and death of CHRIST.

1.

THE LORD's Supper was chiefly ordained for a *Sacrament*. 1. To *represent* the sufferings of CHRIST which are *past*, whereof it is a *memorial*. 2. To *convey* the first-fruits of these sufferings, in *present graces*, whereof it is a means; and 3. To *assure* us of *glory to come*, whereof it is an infallible *pledge*.

2. As this *Sacrament* looks back, it is a *memorial* which our LORD hath left in His Church, of what He was pleased to suffer for her. For though these sufferings of His were both so dreadful and holy, as to make the heavens mourn, the earth quake, and all men tremble: yet because the greatest things are apt to be forgotten when they are gone, therefore He was pleased at His last Supper to ordain this, as a holy *memorial* and *representation* of what He was then about to suffer. So that when Christian

posterity (like the young *Israelites* who had not seen the killing of the first Passover) should come to ask after the meaning of the *bread broken*, the *wine poured* out, and the *partaking* of both : this holy Mystery might set forth both the *martyrdom* and the *sacrifice* of this crucified Saviour; giving up His *Flesh*, shedding His *Blood*, and pouring out His very *soul*, to atone for *their* sins.

3. Therefore, as at the Passover the late Jews could say, *This is the lamb, these are the herbs, our fathers did eat in Egypt;* because these latter feasts did so effectually represent the former: so at our Holy Communion, which sets before our eyes CHRIST *our Passover who is sacrificed for us;* our Saviour, says St. *Austin, doubted not to say, This is my Body, when He gave the disciples the figure of His Body:* especially because this Sacrament, duly received, makes the thing which it represents, as really present for our use as if it were newly done. *Eating this bread, and drinking this cup, ye do shew forth the Lord's death.*

4. And surely, it is no *common* regard we ought to have for these venerable representations, which GOD Himself has set up in, and for His Church. For these are far more than an ordinary figure. And all sorts of *signs* and *monuments* are more or less venerable, according to the things which they represent. And these, besides their ordinary use, bear as it were on their face the glorious character of their Divine appointment, and the express design that GOD hath to revive thereby, and to expose to all

our senses, His sufferings, as if they were present *now*.

5. Ought not then one who looks on these ordinances, and considers the great and dreadful passages which they set before him, to say in his heart, I observe on this Altar somewhat very like the Sacrifice of my Saviour! For thus the *Bread of Life* was broken: thus the *Lamb of God* was slain, and His *Blood* shed. And when I look on the minister who by special order from God distributes this bread and this wine, I conceive, that thus GOD Himself hath both given His Son to die, and gives us still the virtue of His death.

6. Ought he not also to reverence and adore, when he looks towards that good Hand, which has appointed for the use of the Church the *Memorial* of these great things? As the *Israelites* whenever they saw the *cloud* on the Temple, which GOD had hallowed to be the sign of His presence, presently used to throw themselves on their faces, not to worship the cloud, but GOD; so whenever I see these better signs of the glorious mercies of GOD, I will not fail both to remember my LORD who appointed them, and to worship Him whom they represent.

7. To complete this worship, let us exercise such a faith as may answer the great end of this Sacrament. The main intention of CHRIST herein was not the bare *remembrance* of His Passion; but over and above, to invite us to His Sacrifice, not as done and gone many years since, but as to grace and

mercy, still lasting, still *new*, still the same as when it was first offered for us. The Sacrifice of Christ being appointed by the Father for a propitiation that should continue to all ages; and withal being everlasting by the privilege of its own *order*, which is *an unchangeable Priesthood;* and by His worth who offered it, that is, the Blessed *Son of God;* and by the power of *the Eternal Spirit,* through whom it was offered: it must in all respects stand eternal, the same yesterday, to-day, and for ever.

8. Here then, *faith* must be as true a *subsistence* of those things past which we *believe,* as it is of the things yet to come which we *hope* for: by the help of which the believer, being prostrate at the Lord's Table, as at the very foot of His Cross, should with earnest sorrow confess and lament all his sins, which were the nails and spears that pierced his Saviour. We ourselves *have crucified that Just One. Men and brethren, what shall we do?* Let us fall amazed at that stroke of Divine justice, that could not be satisfied but by the death of God! *How dreadful is this place!* How deep and holy is this Mystery! What thanks should we pay for those inconceivable mercies of God the Father, who so gave up His only Son! and for the mercies of God the Son, who thus gave Himself up for us!

9. My Lord and my God, I behold in this Bread, made of corn that was cut down, beaten, ground, and bruised by men, all the heavy blows and plagues and pains which Thou didst suffer from Thy murderers. I behold in this Bread, dried up and baked

with fire, the fiery wrath which Thou didst suffer from above! My GOD, my GOD, why hast Thou forsaken Him? The violence of wicked men first hath made Him a *Martyr;* then the fire of heaven hath made Him a *Burnt-Sacrifice;* and, lo, He has become to me the *Bread of Life!*

Let me go, then, to take and eat it. For though the instruments that bruised Him be broken, and the flames that burnt Him be put out, yet this *Bread* continues new. The spears and swords that slew, and the burnings that completed the Sacrifice, are many years since scattered and spent. But the sweet smell of the Offering still remains, the Blood is still warm, the Wounds still fresh, and *the Lamb* still *standing as slain.* Any other sacrifice by time may lose its strength: but Thou, O Eternal Victim, offered up to GOD through the Eternal Spirit, remainest always the same. And as Thy years shall not fail, so they shall never abate anything of Thy saving strength and mercy. O help me, that they abate nothing of my faith! Help me to grieve for my sins and Thy pains, as they did who saw Thee suffer. Let my heart burn to follow Thee now, when this Bread is broken at this Table, as the hearts of Thy disciples did when Thou didst break it in *Emmaus.* O Rock of *Israel,* Rock of Salvation, Rock struck and cleft for me, let those two streams of *Blood* and *Water,* which once gushed out of Thy side, bring down *pardon* and *holiness* into my soul. And let me thirst after them now, as if I stood upon the mountain whence sprung this *Water;*

and near the *cleft* of that Rock, the wounds of my
LORD, whence gushed this sacred *Blood.* All the
distance of time and countries between *Adam* and
me doth not keep his sin and punishment from
reaching me, any more than if I had been born
in his house. *Adam* descended from above, let Thy
Blood reach as far, and come as freely to save and
sanctify me as the blood of my first father did both
to destroy and to defile me. Blessed JESU, strengthen
my faith, prepare my heart, and then bless Thine
Ordinance. If I but *touch* as I ought *the hem of
Thy garment*—the garment of Thy Passion—virtue
will proceed out of Thee; it shall be done according to my faith, and my poor soul shall be made
whole !

SECTION III.

Concerning the Sacrament as it is a sign of present graces.

1.

AS to the *present graces* that attend the due use of this Sacrament, it is (1) a *figure* whereby GOD *represents ;* (2) an *instrument* whereby He *conveys* them.

First, it is a *figure* or sign thereof. It is the ordinary way of GOD, when He either promises or bestows on men any considerable blessing, to confirm His *word* and His *gift* with the addition of some sign. So the *burning bush* was a *sign* to *Moses,* and the *cloud* that went with them to the *Israelites.* And in like manner hath CHRIST ordained outward visible signs of His inward spiritual grace, to assure every one who believes that he shall be cleansed from his sins as certainly as he sees that *water,* and that he shall be fed with the grace of GOD as certainly as he feeds on the *bread* and *wine.*

2. And as *water* was fitly chosen for the outward sign in *Baptism,* because of the virtue it hath to

cleanse and purify, so were bread and wine fitly chosen for the outward signs of what is represented in the LORD'S Supper; *viz.*, first, the sufferings of CHRIST; and second, the blessings which we receive thereby. First: the sufferings of CHRIST. This bread and wine do not sustain me, till the one has been cut down, ground, and baked with fire, and the other pressed and trodden under foot. Nor did the Son of GOD save me but by being bruised, and pressed, and consumed as it were by the fire of GOD'S wrath. As the best corn is not bread while it stands in the field, so neither could JESUS, living, teaching, working miracles, be the Bread of Life: it must be JESUS suffering, JESUS crucified, JESUS dying. Nothing less than the Cross, than wounds and death, my LORD, my GOD, could of Thy dearest Son make my Saviour!

3. This Sacrament, secondly, represents the blessings which we receive by His Passion. Now, as without bread and wine, or something answerable thereto, the strongest bodies soon decay, so without the virtue of the Body and Blood of CHRIST the holiest souls must soon perish. And as bread and wine keep up our *natural life,* so doth our LORD JESUS, by a continual supply of strength and grace, represented by bread and wine, sustain that *spiritual life* which He hath procured by His Cross.

4. The first breath of spiritual life in our nostrils is the first purchase of CHRIST'S Blood. But, alas! how soon would this first life vanish away, were it not followed and supported by a second! Therefore the Sacrifice of CHRIST procures also grace to

renew and preserve the life He hath given. As the Blood which He shed satisfied the Divine Justice, and removed our punishment, so the water washes and cleanses the pardoned soul; and both these blessings are inseparable, even as the Blood and the Water were which flowed together out of His side.

5. There remains yet another life, which is an absolute redemption from death and our miseries. This, as to the right of it, is together with the other purchased by the same Sacrifice; but as to the possession, it is reserved for us in heaven till CHRIST becomes our full and final redemption. Now the giver of these lives is the preserver of them too; and to this end He sets up a table by His Altar, where He engages to feed our souls with the constant supply of His mercies, as really as He feeds our bodies with this Bread and Wine. In the deliverance from *Egypt* here is a people saved by the sacrifice of the Passover; and lest they should die in the wilderness, there you see an angel leading them with his light, keeping them cool under the shadow of his cloud, and feeding them with manna. JESUS is the Truth foreshewed by these figures. He was the true Passover when He died upon the Cross, and He feeds from heaven, by continually pouring out His blessings, the souls He redeemed by pouring out His Blood.

6. Thus the Sacrament alone represents at once both what our LORD suffered, and what He still doth for us. What we take and eat is made of a sub-

stance cut, bruised, and put to the fire; that shews my Saviour's Passion: and it was used thus that it might afford me food; that shews the benefit I receive from His Passion. In the Sacrament are represented both life and death; the life is mine, the death my Saviour's. O Blessed JESUS, my life comes out of Thy death, and the salvation which I hope for is purchased with all the pain and agonies which Thou didst suffer.

7. Author of my salvation, bestow on me these two blessings which this Sacrament shews together, —mercy, and strength to keep mercy. *Hosanna, O Son of* David, save and preserve! Save me, that I may not fall by the hand of the destroyer; and preserve me, that after this salvation I may not fall by my own hand: but set forward in me, notwithstanding all my sins, the work of Thy faithful mercies. Let me not increase my guilt by abusing what Thou givest. My Saviour, my Preserver, give me always what Thou givest once. Create in me a new heart; but keep what Thou createst, and increase more and more what Thou plantest. O Son of GOD, feed this tender branch, which without Thee cannot but wither; and strengthen Thou a bruised reed, which without Thee cannot but fall. Father of everlasting compassions, forsake not in the wilderness a feeble *Israelite* whom Thou hast brought a little way out of *Egypt;* and let not a poor soul whom Thou hast helped a while ever faint and fall from the right way. Thou art as able to perfect me with the blessings out of Thy throne as to redeem me by the Sacrifice on Thy

Cross. O Thou who art the Truth of what Thou biddest me take, perform in me what Thou dost shew. Give me eternal life by those Thy sufferings; for here is the *Body broken:* give also strength and nourishment for this life; for here is the *Bread of heaven.*

SECTION IV.

Concerning the Sacrament, as it is a means of grace.

1.

HITHERTO we have considered this holy Sacrament both as a *memorial* of the death of CHRIST, and a sign of those graces wherewith He sustains and nourishes believing souls. But this is not all; for both the end of the Holy Communion, the wants and desires of those who receive it, and the strength of other places of the Scripture, require that much more be contained therein than a bare *memorial* or *representation*. (1.) The end of the Holy Communion, which is to make us partakers of CHRIST in another manner than when we only hear His word. (2.) The wants and desires of those who receive it, who seek not a bare *representation* or *remembrance*. I want and seek my Saviour Himself, and I haste to this Sacrament for the same purpose that SS. *Peter* and *John* hasted to His sepulchre—because I hope to find Him there. (3.) The strength of other places of Scripture, which allow it a far greater virtue than that so representing only. *The cup of blessing, which we bless, is it not the Communion of the Blood of Christ?* A *means* of communicating the Blood there represented and remembered to every believing soul!

2. And that it doth convey grace and blessing to the true believer, is evident from its conveying a curse to the profane. *Whosoever eateth unworthily,* saith St. *Paul, eateth damnation to himself.* And how can we think that it is thus really hurtful when abused, but not really blissful in its right use; or that this Bread should be *effectual* to procure death, but not *effectual* to procure salvation? GOD forbid that the Body of CHRIST, who came to save, not destroy, should not shed as much of its *savour of life* to the devout soul, as it doth of its *savour of death* to the wicked and impenitent!

3. I come then to GOD's Altar, with a full persuasion that these words, *This is my Body,* promise me more than a *figure;* that this holy Banquet is not a bare *memorial* only, but may actually *convey* as many blessings to me, as it brings curses on the profane receiver. Indeed, in what manner this is done, I know not; it is enough for me to admire. *One thing I know,* (as said the blind man of our LORD,) *He laid clay upon mine eyes, and behold I see.* He hath blessed, and given me this Bread, and my soul receiveth comfort. I know that clay hath nothing in itself, which could have wrought such a miracle. And I know that this Bread hath nothing in itself, which can impart grace, holiness, and sal-

vation. But I know also, that it is the ordinary way of God to produce His greatest works at the presence, though not by the power, of the most useless instruments. At the very stroke of a rod He divided the sea. At the blowing some trumpets He threw down massive walls. At the washing in *Jordan* He cured *Naaman* of a plague that was naturally incurable. And when but a shadow went by, or some oil was dropped, or clothes were touched by those that were sick, presently *virtue went out ;* not of rods, or trumpets, or shadows, or clothes—but of Himself.

4. It was the right hand of the Lord which of old time brought these mighty things to pass, either when the Red Sea opened a way for *Israel* to march, or when the rock poured out rivers to refresh them. And so now it is Christ Himself, with His Body and Blood, once offered to God upon the Cross, and ever since standing before Him as slain, who fills His Church with the perfumes of His Sacrifice, whence faithful communicants return home with the first-fruits of salvation. Bread and wine can contribute no more to it than the rod of *Moses* or the oil of the apostles. But yet since it pleaseth Christ to work thereby, O my God, whensoever Thou shalt bid me *go and wash in* Jordan, I will go ; and will no more doubt of being made clean from my sins, than if I had bathed in Thy Blood. And when Thou sayest, *Go, take and eat this Bread* which I have blessed, I will doubt no more of being fed with the Bread of Life, than if I were eating Thy very flesh.

5. This Victim having been offered up in the fulness of times, and in the midst of the world, which is Christ's great temple, and having been thence carried up to heaven, which is His sanctuary; from thence spreads salvation all around, as the burnt-offering did its smoke. And thus His Body and Blood have everywhere, but especially at this Sacrament, a true and real Presence. When He offered Himself upon earth, the vapour of His Atonement went up and darkened the very sun; and, by rending the great veil, it clearly shewed He had made a way into heaven. And, since He is gone up, He sends down to earth the graces that spring continually both from His everlasting Sacrifice and from the continual intercession that attends it. So that we need not say, *Who will go up into heaven?* since, without either ascending or descending, this sacred Body of Jesus fills with atonement and blessing the remotest part of this temple.

6. Of these blessings Christ from above is pleased to bestow sometimes more, sometimes less, in the several ordinances of His Church, which, as the stars in heaven, differ from each other in glory. Fasting, prayer, hearing His word, are all good vessels to draw water from this well of salvation; but they are not all equal. The Holy Communion, when well used, exceeds as much in blessing as it exceeds in danger of a curse, when wickedly and irreverently taken.

7. This great and holy Mystery communicates to us the death of our Blessed Lord, both as *offering*

Himself to God, and as giving Himself to man. As He *offered Himself to God*, it enters me into that mystical body for which He died, and which is dead with CHRIST: yea, it sets me on the very shoulders of that Eternal Priest, while He offers up Himself, and intercedes for His spiritual *Israel*. And by this means it conveys to me the *communion of His Sufferings*, which leads to a communion in all His graces and glories. *As He offers Himself to man*, the Holy Sacrament is, after the sacrifice for sin, the true sacrifice of peace-offerings, and the table purposely set to receive those mercies that are sent down from His Altar. *Take and eat ; this is My Body, which was broken for you ; and this is My Blood, which was shed for you.*

8. Here then I wait at the LORD's Table, which both *shews* me what an Apostle, who had heaven for his school, had the greatest mind to see and learn, and *offers* me the richest gift which a saint can receive on earth, the *Lord Jesus crucified.*

Amen, my LORD and my GOD ! Give me all which Thou shewest, and grant that I may faithfully keep all Thou givest. Bless Thine Ordinance, and make it an effectual means of Thy grace; then bless and sanctify my heart also. O my Father, here I offer up to Thee my soul ; and Thou offerest to me Thy Son. What I offer is indeed an unclean habitation to receive the *Holy One of Israel.* Come in, nevertheless, Thou Eternal Priest ; but cleanse my house at Thy coming. I am a poor, sinful, lost creature ; but, such as I am, sinful and lost, I wait for Thy salvation. Come in, O Lord, with Thy salvation to a dying man, and make me whole; to a sinner bound hand and foot, and release me. Come as Thou didst to the publican. Oh, let this day salvation come to this house.

SECTION V.

Concerning the Sacrament, as it is a pledge of future glory.

1.

A PLEDGE and an EARNEST differ in this, that an *earnest* may be allowed upon *account* for part of that payment which is promised, whereas *pledges* are taken back. Thus, for example, zeal, love, and those degrees of holiness which GOD bestows in the use of His Sacraments, will remain with us when we are in heaven, and there make part of our happiness. But the Sacraments themselves shall be taken back, and shall no more appear in heaven than did the cloudy pillar in *Canaan*. We shall have no need of these sacred *figures* of Christ when we see Him face to face, or of these *pledges* of that glory to be revealed when we shall actually possess it. But till this day the Holy Sacrament hath that third use, of being a *pledge* from the LORD that He will give us that glory.

2. Our LORD pointed at this when He said to His

disciples, the Holy Cup being in His hand, that He would *drink no more of that fruit till He should drink it new in the kingdom of His Father.* In the purpose of God, His Church and heaven go both together, that being the way that leads to this, as the holy place to the holiest, both which are implied in what *Christ* calls the *kingdom of God.* Whosoever, therefore, are admitted to this *Dinner* of the Lamb, unless they be wanting to themselves, need not doubt of being admitted to the Marriage Supper of Him Who was dead, but *now liveth for evermore.*

3. Our Saviour hath given us by His death three kinds of life, and He promises to nourish us in every one of them by these tokens of bread and wine which He hath made His Sacrament. Two of these are already nourished hereby, but to the third we are not yet come. This is that eternal life for which we are as yet too vile vessels. We are now neither of age to enjoy our inheritance, nor able to bear the weight of eternal glory; and therefore it lies for us in His hands. But we *know in Whom we have believed, and are persuaded He is able to keep that safe which we have committed unto Him against that day.* By faith we deposit or lay down this great treasure in the hands of God to keep; and God, by this Sacrament, assures us both that He will keep it safe and will restore it to us when we are meet for it.

4. This third use is the crown of the other two; and, indeed, they all aim at the same glory. The first is, to set out as new and fresh the holy sufferings

which purchased our title to eternal happiness; the second is, both to represent and to convey to our souls all necessary graces to qualify us for it; and the third is, to assure us that when we are qualified for it, God will faithfully render to us the purchase. And these three make up the proper sense of those words, *Take, eat ; this is My Body.* For the consecrated Bread doth not only represent His Body, and bring the virtue of it into our souls on earth, but as to our happiness in heaven, bought with that price, it is the most solemn instrument to assure our title to it.

5. Our Blessed LORD, being desirous before His death, as by a deed of His last will, to settle on His disciples both such a measure of grace in this life as might now make them holy, and after this life such a fulness of blessings as might make them eternally happy, He delivers into our hands, by way of instrument and conveyance, the blessed Sacrament of His Body and Blood, in the same manner as kings used to bestow dignities by the bestowing of a *staff* or a *sword*, and as the fathers bestow estates on their children by giving them some few *writings*.

6. The reason of all this is, the giver cannot put into his friend's hands houses and lands, because they are of an immoveable nature. And therefore this must be supplied by some forms or tokens by which his design may be sufficiently made known. Now CHRIST, and His estate, His happiness and His glory, His eternity and His heaven, are not things that may be moved more easily than the mountains on the earth; and therefore these can be no other-

wise made over than great immoveable estates are. Wherefore, as the kingdom of *Israel* was once made over to *David*, with the oil that *Samuel* poured upon his head, so the Body and Blood of JESUS is *in full value*, and heaven with all its glory *in sure title*, made over to true Christians by that bread and wine which they receive in the Holy Communion, the minister of CHRIST having as much power from his Master for doing this as any prophet ever had for what he did.

7. O LORD JESU, who hast ordained these Mysteries for a communion of Thy Body, a means of Thy grace, and a pledge of Thy glory, settle me hereby in the communion of Thy sufferings which they *shew forth;* feed me with that Living Bread which they *present*, and sanctify me in body and spirit for that eternal happiness which they *promise*.

Eternal Priest, who art gone up on high to receive gifts for men, fill my heart, I beseech Thee, with blessings out of Thy holy seat, as now Thou fillest my mouth with the holy things of Thy Church. O that in the strength of this Meat I may walk my forty days, till I come to that holy mountain where, without the help of any bread or outward sign, I shall see my GOD face to face! Blessed Spirit, help me to drink so worthily of this fruit of the vine that I may drink it new in the kingdom of my Father!

SECTION VI.

Concerning the Sacrament, as it is a Sacrifice. And first, of the Commemorative Sacrifice.

1.

THERE never was on earth a true religion without some kind of sacrifices. And the heathens who cast this slander on the Christian Church, did it for no better reason than this, because they saw neither altars set up, nor beasts slain or burnt among them. Even as they accused the Jews of adoring nothing but clouds, because they had no gods of stone or silver. Whereas in truth, as what was stone or silver could not be a god; so neither could the bare slaughter of beasts be a real sacrifice. None of these sacrifices could ever take away sin, but in dependence on that of JESUS CHRIST. And no sacrifice under the law could represent our service to GOD so fully as it is done under the gospel. The Holy Communion alone brings together these two great ends, atonement of sins, and acceptable duty to GOD, of which all the sacrifices of old were no more than weak shadows. As for the atonement of sin, 'tis sure the Sacrifice of CHRIST alone was sufficient for it. And that this great Sacrifice, being both of an infinite value, to satisfy the most severe justice, and of an infinite virtue, to produce all its effects at once, need never more be repeated. This perhaps was the want of faith in *Moses* (Numb. xx. 12); to strike a second time, and without order, that mysterious rock, which to strike once had been enough. For this second blow could only proceed from a faithless mistrust, as if the first, which alone was enjoined, could not suffice. But it were a much greater offence against the Blood of CHRIST, to question its infinite worth. The offering of it, therefore, must needs be one only; and the repeating thereof utterly superfluous.

2. Nevertheless this Sacrifice, which by a *real* oblation was not to be offered more than once, is, by a devout and thankful commemoration, to be offered up every day. This is what the Apostle calls, *To set forth the death of the* LORD; To set it forth as well before the eyes of GOD His Father, as before the eyes of men: And what St. Austin *explained* when he said, "The holy Flesh of JESUS was offered in three manners, by *prefiguring sacrifices* under the law before His coming into the world, in *real deed* upon His Cross, and by a *commemorative Sacrament* after He ascended into Heaven. All comes to this, (1) That the *Sacrifice* in itself can never be repeated; (2) That nevertheless, this Sacrament, by our remembrance, becomes a kind of *Sacrifice*, whereby

we present before GOD the Father that precious Oblation of His Son once offered. And thus do we every day offer unto GOD the meritorious sufferings of our LORD, as the only sure ground whereon GOD may give, and we obtain, the blessings we pray for. Now there is no ordinance or mystery that is so blessed an instrument to reach this everlasting Sacrifice, and to set it solemnly forth before the eyes of GOD, as the Holy Communion is. *To men* it is a *sacred Table* where GOD's minister is ordered to represent from GOD his Master the Passion of His dear Son, as still fresh, and still powerful for their eternal salvation. And *to* GOD it is an *Altar* whereon men mystically present to Him the same Sacrifice as still bleeding and suing for mercy. And because it is the High Priest Himself, the true anointed of the LORD, who hath set up both this Table and the Altar, for the communication of His Body and Blood to men, and for the representation of both to GOD; it cannot be doubted but that the one is most profitable to the penitent sinner, and the other most acceptable to His gracious Father.

3. The people of *Israel*, in worshipping, ever turned their eyes and their hearts toward that sacrifice, the blood whereof the high-priest was to carry into the sanctuary. So let us ever turn our eyes and our hearts toward JESUS our eternal High Priest, who is gone up into the true sanctuary, and doth there continually present both His own Body and Blood before GOD, and, as *Aaron* did, all the true *Israel* of GOD in a *memorial*. In the meantime,

we beneath in the Church present to GOD His Body and Blood in a *memorial*, that under the shadow of His Cross, and figure of His Sacrifice, we may present ourselves in very deed before Him.

4. O LORD, who seest nothing in me that is truly mine, but sinful dust and ashes, look upon the Sacrifice of Thy dear Son, once offered for my sins. Turn Thine eyes, O merciful Father, to the satisfaction and intercession of my LORD, who now sits at Thy right hand; to the Seals of Thy Covenant which lie before Thee upon this Table; and to all the wants, weaknesses, and distresses which Thou seest in my heart. O Father, glorify Thy Son; O Son of GOD, bless Thou Thine Ordinance, and send with it the influences of that Spirit whom Thou hast promised to all flesh; that, by the help of these mercies, the world, the Church, and our souls may glorify Thee now and ever.

SECTION VII.

Concerning the Sacrifice of ourselves.

1.

TOO many who are called Christians live as if under the Gospel there were no sacrifice but that of CHRIST on the Cross. And indeed there is no other that can atone for our sins or satisfy the justice of GOD. Though the whole Church should offer up herself as a burnt sacrifice to GOD, yet could she contribute no more towards bearing away the wrath to come, than those who stood near CHRIST when He gave up the ghost, did toward the darkening of the sun or the shaking of the earth. But what is not necessary to this Sacrifice which alone redeemed mankind, is absolutely necessary to our having a share in that redemption. So that though the sacrifice of ourselves cannot *procure* salvation, yet it is altogether needful to our *receiving* it.

2. As *Aaron* never came in before the LORD without the whole people of *Israel*, represented both by the twelve stones on his breast and by the two others

on his shoulder; so JESUS CHRIST does nothing without His Church, insomuch that sometimes they are represented as only one person; seeing CHRIST acts and suffers for His Body in that manner which becomes the Head, and the Church follows all the motions and sufferings of her Head, in such a manner as is possible to its weak members.

3. The whole divinity of St. *Paul* turns upon this *conformity* both of actions and sufferings; and that of St. *John* likewise, upon this same *communion* or fellowship. The truth is, our LORD had neither birth, nor death, nor resurrection on earth, but such as we are to *conform* to; as He had neither ascension, nor everlasting life, nor glory in heaven, but such as we may have in *common* with Him.

4. This *conformity* to CHRIST, which is the grand principle of the whole Christian religion, relates first to our duty about His *sufferings*, and then to our happiness about His *exaltation*, presupposing His *sufferings*. And both make up a full comment on our LORD's frequent command to His disciples to *follow Him*. For without doubt we shall follow Him into heaven, if we will follow Him on earth; and shall have *communion* with Him in glory, if we have *conformity* with Him here in His *sufferings*.

5. These expressions, to *follow*, to have *conformity*, and to have *communion*, oblige us all to follow Him as much as in us lies, through all the parts of His life, and every function of His office. We must be born with Him, die on His Cross, be buried in His grave, suffer in His tribulations. *Christ* and Christians

must be continually together: *Where I am*, saith He, *there shall My servant be.* But of all these duties, the most necessary is the bearing of His Cross, and dying with Him in *Sacrifice.*

6. CHRIST never designed to offer Himself for His people, without His people, no more than the high-priests of old. He presented Himself to GOD in this great temple, the world, at the head of whole mankind. He came as a voluntary Victim to the Altar, being attended on by His *Israel*, who, as it were, with their hands, laid all their sins upon His head. Therefore, as it was necessary that they who sought for atonement should wait upon the sacrifice, so it is, that whoever seeks eternal salvation should wait at that Altar, the Cross, whereon this eternal Priest and Sacrifice was pleased to offer up Himself.

7. The sinners indeed under the law did not die at the altar, the victim alone being burned and destroyed. But because they laid their hands on it when it was dying, and fell on their faces to the ground when it fell bleeding to death, they were reputed to *offer* up themselves as well as the victim. So Christians are not crucified in the same manner as CHRIST was; yet because they cast themselves upon His Cross and sufferings as the only means of atonement for their sins, and salvation for their souls; because of the grief they suffer to think of the Son of GOD thus dying, dying only for their sake, which is as a sword both to pierce their hearts and pierce and crucify their sins; and because their whole body of sin being thus crucified, there remains no life in

them, but what is offered up to God's service. On all these grounds, the Saviour thus offering Himself, and the saved so united to Him by faith, so partaking of His sufferings, and so given up to His will, are accounted before God one and the same Sacrifice.

8. But be it observed, that in order to their being so accounted, they are to crucify their sinful members as really as Christ Himself had His sinless Body crucified; so that each may say, *I am crucified to the world, and the world crucified to me.* And thus Jesus Christ and His whole Church do together make up that complete Sacrifice which was fore-shewn by that of old, whereof the kidney and fat were burnt upon the altar; but the flesh, the skin, feet, and dung—emblems of sin—were thrown and burnt without the camp. For Christ and His Church so join in one Offering, that He contributes all that can go up into heaven to appease and please God; and we contribute nothing but sin, but what must be removed out of the way; yea, and so that it is needful further, in order to our being accounted one Sacrifice with Him, that not only our persons, but all our actions likewise, be wholly devoted to God. *I am crucified with Christ; now I live not,* saith the Christian, *but Christ liveth in me. And the life which I now live in the flesh, I live by faith in the Son of God.*

9. This act of the Church consecrating herself to God, and so joined to Christ, as to make but one Oblation with Him, is the Mystery which was once

represented by the daily sacrifice ; the first and chief part whereof was the lamb, which did foreshew the Lamb of God ; the second was the *meat*—or rather *meal*—and *drink-offering*, made of flour, mingled with oil and wine ; all which being thrown on the lamb continually, was accounted one and the same sacrifice. Now these, which were so thrown on the main sacrifice, signified properly these offerings which Christians must present to God of themselves, their goods and their praises. From this *meal* and *drink-offering* came the bread and wine to be used at the Lord's Supper. Now all we can offer on our own account is but such an oblation as this *meal* and *drink-offering* was, which cannot be presented alone, but only with the merits of Jesus Christ, and which cannot go to heaven but with the smoke of that Great Burnt Sacrifice. On the one side, neither our persons nor works can be presented to God, otherwise than as these additional offerings, which of themselves fall to the ground, unless the Great Sacrifice sustain them. And on the other side, this Great Sacrifice sustains and sanctifies only those things that are thrown into His fire, hallowed upon His Altar, and together with Him consecrated to God.

10. Now though we are called at all times to this *conformity* and *communion* in the sufferings of Christ, yet more especially when we approach this dreadful Mystery let us take a peculiar care, that as both the principal and additional sacrifices went up towards heaven in the same flame, so Jesus Christ and all

His members may jointly appear before God, that we may offer up our souls and bodies, at the same time, in the same place, and in the same Oblation. Let us take care to attend on this Sacrifice in such a manner (1) as may become faithful disciples, who are resolved to die for and with their Master; (2) as true members that cannot outlive their Head; and (3) as penitent sinners, who cannot look for any share in the glory of their Saviour, unless they really enter into the communion of that Sacrifice and those sufferings which their Master, their Head, and their Saviour has passed through, and which they are engaged to by this very Sacrament.

11. To this effect, the faithful worshipper, presenting that soul and body, which God hath given him, at the Altar, may say,—

Lo, I come! if this soul and body may be useful to anything, *to do Thy will*, O God. And if it please Thee to use the power that Thou hast over dust and ashes, over weak flesh and blood, over a brittle vessel of clay, over the work of Thine own hands; lo, here they are, to suffer also Thy good pleasure. If Thou please to visit me with either pain or dishonour, I will *humble myself* under it, and, through Thy grace, be *obedient unto death, even the death upon the Cross.* Whatsoever may befall me, either from neighbours or strangers, since it is Thou employest them, though they know it not (unless Thou help me to some lawful means of redressing the wrong), I will not *open my mouth before the* Lord who smiteth me, except only to sing the *Psalm* after

I have eaten those bitter herbs which belong to this *Passover*, and to *bless the* LORD. Hereafter no man can take away anything from me, no life, no honour, no estate: since I am ready to lay them down, as soon as I perceive Thou requirest them at my hands. Nevertheless, *O Father, if Thou be willing, remove this cup from me; but if not, Thy will be done.* Whatever sufferings hereafter may trouble my flesh, or whatever agonies may trouble my spirit, *O Father, into Thy hand will I commend* my life, and all that concerneth it. And if Thou be pleased, either that I live yet awhile, or not, I will with my Saviour *bow down my head;* I will humble myself under Thy hand; I will give up all Thou art pleased to ask, until at last I *give up the ghost.*

12. O GOD and Father, bestow on me such a measure of that *Spirit, through* which Thy Son *offered Himself,* as may sanctify for ever the body and soul which I now offer: a spirit of contrition, that I may loathe those sins which delivered my GOD to death; and a spirit of holiness, that I may never be tempted to them again, any more than a crucified man can be tempted. O let this body never be untied from His Cross, to return afresh to folly and vanity. Arm and rod of the LORD, who didst revenge my sins on Thy own Son, correct and destroy them also in me. O my GOD, accept of a heart that sheds now before Thee its tears, as a poor victim does its blood; and that raises up unto Thee all its desires, as a burnt-offering does its flames. And since my sacrifice can neither be holy nor

accepted, being alone, receive it, O Father, clothed with the righteousness of Thy Son, and made acceptable with that holy perfume which rises from off His Altar: and grant that He who sanctifies, and they who are sanctified, may partake of one Passion, and enjoy with Thee the same glory.

SECTION VIII.

Concerning the Sacrifice of our goods.

1.

T is an express command of GOD by *Moses*, that no worshipper should appear before the LORD empty. Nor is this repealed by CHRIST. Sincere Christians therefore, at the receiving of the Holy Communion, should, together with the actual *sacrifice* of themselves, bring the *free-will offering* of their goods. Indeed, this as naturally follows the former, as the fruits and leaves follow the tree, and as what we *have* or *can* do comes after what we *are*. Otherwise, our sacrifice were maimed, and would not suit with that of CHRIST, which was whole and entire. Therefore, as our bodies and souls are sacrifices attending the sacrifice of CHRIST, so must all our goods attend the sacrifice of our persons. In a word, whensoever we offer ourselves, we offer, by the self-same act, all that we *have*, all that we *can* do, and therein engage for all, that it shall be dedicated to the glory of GOD, and that it shall be surrendered into His hands, and employed for such uses as He shall appoint.

2. It behoved *Israel* to go forth out of *Egypt* with all their cattle and goods, to offer them unto the Lord, that He might take either all, or such a part, as He would be pleased to choose. And so it behoves every sinner at his conversion to God, and whenever he approaches His Table, to consecrate all he has to Jesus Christ. From that very moment that we give up ourselves to Christ, who hath likewise given Himself for us, as all He possesses becomes ours, namely, His grace, His immortality, His glory, which he bestows upon us at the times He sees best for our salvation; so all we have becomes His, and He may take it after, in what time and manner He shall see best for His glory. All things are His, as He is sovereign Lord and God. But all we have is His by a further title, because we have given them, with our own persons, by our own act and deed. So that all which we are, which we can give, even to the least vessel in our houses, is made holy in this one consecration, according to the words of the prophet, *In that day shall be upon the very bridles of the horses, Holiness unto the* Lord ; *and every pot in* Jerusalem *and* Judah *shall be holy unto the* Lord (Zech. xiv. 20, 21).

3. This consecration, whereby the worshipper offers up himself and all his concerns to God, is first, as to our souls and bodies, an inexpressible blessing, raising us to the very nature, the holiness, and immortality of God. Secondly, as to the consecrated things, it is a miraculous privilege, which infinitely multiplies whatever is thus parted with.

It blesses the use of it, although it be but presented, as long as we can enjoy it : and exchanges it, when we can enjoy it no more, not as if water was turned into wine, or dirt into gold ; but as if we conceive a glass of water turned into streams of everlasting comforts, small cottages of clay into royal palaces, or the dust of *Israel* into so many stars of heaven.

4. Now though our LORD, by that everlasting Sacrifice of Himself, offers Himself at all times and in all places, as we likewise offer ourselves and all that is ours, to be a continual sacrifice ; yet because CHRIST offers Himself for us at the Holy Communion, in a peculiar manner ; we also should then, in a more special manner, renew all our sacrifices. Then and there, at the Altar of GOD, it is right both to repeat all the vows and promises which for some hindrance or other we had not yet the convenience to fulfil ; and to renew all those other performances which can never be fulfilled but with the end of our days.

5. But at the same time that the Christian believer does any good work, let him draw out of the good measure of his heart *fire* and *frankincense*, that is, such zeal and love as may raise good, *moral* works into religious sacrifices. Whenever he helps his neighbour, let him so reverently and fervently lift up his heart to God, as may become both that Majesty he adores, and the pious act which he intends. And then whether he do it at his door, or in the way, or in the temple, it matters not ; for the hour is long since come, that acts of religion are not confined

either to *Jerusalem*, or *to this mountain.* Whereso-ever thou hast the occasion of doing a holy work, there GOD makes *holy ground* for thee : only in order to become a spiritual worshipper, the work must be done *in spirit and in truth :* with such a mind and thought, with such faith and love, as though thou wert laying thy *oblation* upon the altar, where thou knowest that CHRIST will both effectually find, and graciously accept it.

6. I dare appear before the LORD, with all my sins and my sorrows. It is just also that I should appear with these few blessings. *Having* received them of Thy hand, now do I offer them to Thee again. For-give, I beseech Thee, my sins, deliver me from my sorrows, and accept of this my sacrifice : or rather look, in my behalf, on that only true Sacrifice, whereof here is the Sacrament ; the Sacrifice of Thy well-beloved Son, proceeding from Thee, to die for me. O let Him come unto me now, as the only begotten of the Father, full of grace and truth !

CHISWICK PRESS:—CHARLES WHITTINGHAM, TOOKS COURT,
CHANCERY LANE.

ON THE
Lord's Supper.

By *JOHN WESLEY*, M. A.

FELLOW of LINCOLN-COLLEGE, OXFORD;

AND

CHARLES WESLEY, M. A.

STUDENT of CHRIST-CHURCH, OXFORD;

With a PREFACE, concerning

The *Christian Sacrament* and *Sacrifice*.

Extracted from Dr. BREVINT.

THE TENTH EDITION.

This do in Remembrance of Me. 1 Cor. xi. 24.

LONDON:

Printed by G. PARAMORE, North-Green, Worship-
Street; and sold by G. WHITFIELD, at the Chapel, City-
Road; and at the Method:ft Preaching-Houses in Town
and Country. 1794.
[*Fac-simile.*]

HYMNS

ON

The Lord's Supper.

I. *As it is a Memorial of the Sufferings and Death of* CHRIST.

HYMN I.

1

IN that sad memorable night,
When JESUS was for us betray'd,
He left His death-recording rite,
He took, and bless'd, and brake the Bread,
And gave His own their last bequest,
And thus His love's intent exprest:

2 Take, eat: this is My Body, given
To purchase life and peace for you,
Pardon and holiness in heaven:
Do this, My dying love to shew;
Accept your precious legacy,
And thus, My friends, remember Me.

3 He took into His hands the Cup,
To crown the Sacramental Feast,
And full of kind concern look'd up,
And gave what He to them had blest;
And drink ye all of This, He said,
In solemn memory of the dead.

4 This is My Blood which seals the new
Eternal covenant of My grace;
My Blood so freely shed for you,
For you and all the sinful race;
My Blood, that speaks your sins forgiven,
And justifies your claim to heaven.

5 The grace which I to all bequeath
In this Divine Memorial take;
And mindful of your Saviour's death,
Do this, My followers, for My sake,
Whose dying love hath left behind
Eternal life for all mankind.

HYMN II.

1 IN this expressive Bread I see
The wheat by man cut down for me,
And beat, and bruis'd, and ground:
The heavy plagues and pains and blows
Which JESUS suffer'd from His foes,
Are in this emblem found.

2 The bread dried up and burnt with fire
  Presents the Father's vengeful ire
    Which my Redeemer bore :
  Into His bones the fire He sent,
  Till all the flaming darts were spent,
    And Justice ask'd no more.

3 Why hast Thou, LORD, forsook Thine own ?
  Alas, what evil hath He done,
    The spotless Lamb of GOD ?
  Cut off, not for Himself, but me,
  He bears my sins on yonder tree,
    And pays my debt in blood.

4 Seiz'd by the rage of sinful man,
  I see Him bound, and bruis'd, and slain ;
    'Tis done, the Martyr dies !
  His life to ransom ours is given,
  And, lo ! the fiercest fire of heaven
    Consumes the Sacrifice.

5 He suffers both from man and GOD,
  He bears the universal load
    Of guilt and misery ;
  He suffers to reverse our doom ;
  And lo ! my LORD is here become
    The Bread of Life to me.

HYMN III.

1 THEN let us go, and take, and eat
 The heavenly everlasting Meat,
  For fainting souls prepar'd;
Fed with the living Bread divine,
Discern we in the sacred sign
  The Body of the LORD.

2 The instruments that bruis'd Him so
Were broke and scatter'd long ago,
  The flames extinguish'd were;
But JESU's death is ever new;
He whom in ages past they slew,
  Doth still as slain appear.

3 The Oblation sends as sweet a smell,
Ev'n now it pleases GOD as well
  As when it first was made:
The Blood doth now as freely flow
As when His side receiv'd the blow
  That shew'd Him newly dead.

4 Then let our faith adore the Lamb
To-day as yesterday the same,
  In Thy great Offering join,
Partake the Sacrificial Food,
And eat Thy Flesh, and drink Thy Blood,
  And live for ever Thine.

HYMN IV.

1   LET all who truly bear
      The bleeding Saviour's name,
Their faithful hearts with us prepare,
    And eat the Paschal Lamb.
    Our Passover was slain
    At *Salem's* hallow'd place,
Yet we who in our tents remain
    Shall gain His largest grace.

2   This Eucharistic Feast
    Our every want supplies,
And still we by His death are blest,
    And share His Sacrifice :
    By faith His Flesh we eat,
    Who here His Passion show,
And GOD out of His holy seat
    Shall all His gifts bestow.

3   Who thus our faith employ
    His sufferings to record,
Ev'n now we mournfully enjoy
    Communion with our LORD,
    As though we every one
    Beneath His Cross had stood,
And seen Him heave, and heard Him groan,
    And felt His gushing Blood.

4 O GOD! 'tis finish'd now!
The mortal pang is past!
By faith His head we see Him bow,
 And hear Him breathe His last!
We too with Him are dead,
 And shall with Him arise;
The Cross on which He bows His head,
 Shall lift us to the skies.

HYMN V.

1 O THOU eternal Victim slain,
 A Sacrifice for guilty man,
By the eternal Spirit made
An Offering in the sinner's stead:
Our everlasting Priest art Thou,
And plead'st Thy death for sinners now.

2 Thy Offering still continues new;
Thy vesture keeps its bloody hue;
Thou stand'st the ever slaughter'd Lamb;
Thy Priesthood still remains the same;
Thy years, O GOD, can never fail;
Thy goodness is unchangeable.

3 O that our faith may never move,
But stand unshaken as Thy love!
Sure evidence of things unseen,
Now let it pass the years between,
And view Thee bleeding on the tree,
My GOD who dies for me, for me!

HYMN VI.

1 AII, give me, LORD, my sins to mourn,
    My sins which have Thy Body torn ;
Give me with broken heart to see
Thy last tremendous agony :
To weep o'er an expiring GOD,
And mix my sorrows with Thy Blood.

2 O could I gain the mountain's height,
And look upon that piteous sight !
O that with *Salem's* daughters, I
Might stand and see my Saviour die,
Smite on my breast, and inly mourn,
But never from Thy Cross return !

HYMN VII.

1 COME, Holy Ghost, set to Thy seal,
    Thine inward witness give ;
To all our waiting souls reveal
    The death by which we live.

2 Spectators of the pangs divine,
    O that we now may be,
Discerning in the sacred sign
    His Passion on the tree !

3 Give us to hear the dreadful sound
    Which told His mortal pain,
Tore up the graves, and shook the ground,
    And rent the rocks in twain.

4 Repeat the Saviour's dying cry
    In every heart, so loud
That every heart may now reply,
    This was the Son of God !

HYMN VIII.

1   COME to the Supper, come,
        Sinners, there still is room ;
Every soul may be His guest,
Jesus gives the general word ;
Share the monumental Feast,
Eat the Supper of your Lord.

2   In this authentic sign
        Behold the stamp divine :
Christ revives His sufferings here,
Still exposes them to view ;
See the Crucified appear,
Now believe He died for you !

HYMN IX.

1 COME hither all, whose groveling taste
    Enslaves your souls, and lays them waste;
     Save your expense, and mend your cheer:
  Here GOD Himself's prepar'd and drest,
  Himself vouchsafes to be your Feast,
     In whom alone all dainties are.

2 Come hither all, whom tempting wine
  Bows to your father *Belial's* shrine,
     Sin all your boast, and sense your god:
  Weep now for what ye've drank amiss,
  And lose your taste of sensual bliss
     By drinking here your Saviour's Blood.

3 Come hither all, whom searching pain,
  And conscience's loud cries arraign,
     Producing all your sins to view:
  Taste, and dismiss your guilty fear,
  O taste, and see that GOD is here,
     To heal your souls, and sin subdue.

4 Come hither all, whom careless joy
  Doth with alluring force destroy,
     While loose ye range beyond your bounds:
  True love is here, that passes quite,
  And all your transient mean delight
     Drowns as a flood the lower grounds.

5 Come hither all, whose idol-love,
While fond the pleasing pain ye prove,
    Raises your foolish raptures high.
True Love is here, whose dying breath
Gave life to us; who tasted death,
    And dying once, no more can die.

6 LORD, I have now invited all:
And instant still the guest shall call,
    Still shall I all invite to Thee:
For, O my GOD, it seems but right
In mine, Thy meanest servant's sight,
    That where all is, there all should be.

HYMN X.

1 FATHER, Thy own in CHRIST receive,
    Who deeply for our follies grieve,
    And cast our sins away:
Resolv'd to lead our lives anew,
Thine only glory to pursue,
    And only Thee obey.

2 Faith in Thy pardoning love we have;
Willing Thou art our souls to save,
    For JESU's sake alone:
JESUS Thy wrath hath pacified,
JESUS, Thy well-belov'd, hath died
    For all mankind to atone.

3 The death sustain'd for all mankind
With humblest thanks we call to mind,
    With grateful joy approve:
And every soul of man embrace,
And love the dearly ransom'd race
    In the Redeemer's love.

4 Receive us then, Thou pardoning GOD,
Partakers of His Flesh and Blood
    Grant that we now may be;
The Spirit's attesting seal impart,
And speak to every sinner's heart,
    The Saviour died for thee!

HYMN XI.

1 . O GOD, that hear'st the prayer,
    Attend Thy people's cry,
Who to Thy house repair,
And on Thy death rely,
Thy death which now we call to mind,
And trust our legacies to find.

2   Thou meetest them that joy
    In these Thy ways to go,
    And to Thy praise employ
    Their happy lives below,
And still within Thy temple-gate
For all Thy promis'd mercies wait.

3   We wait to obtain them now,
We seek the Crucified,
And at Thy Altar bow;
And long to feel applied
The Blood for our redemption given,
And eat the Bread that came from heaven.

4   Come then, our dying LORD,
To us Thy goodness show,
In honour of Thy word
The inward grace bestow,
And magnify the sacred sign,
And prove the Ordinance divine.

HYMN XII.

1 JESU, suffering Deity,
    Can we help remembering Thee?·
Thee, whose Blood for us did flow;
Thee, who diedst to save Thy foe.

2 Thee, Redeemer of mankind,
Gladly now we call to mind,
Thankfully Thy grace approve,
Take the tokens of Thy love.

3 This for Thy dear sake we do,
Here Thy bloody Passion shew,
Till Thou dost to judgment come,
Till Thy arms receive us home.

4 Then we walk in means no more,
  There their sacred use is o'er,
  There we see Thee face to face,
  Saved eternally by grace.

HYMN XIII.

1 COME, all who truly bear
    The name of CHRIST your LORD,
His last mysterious Supper share,
  And keep His kindest word:
  Hereby your faith approve,
  In JESUS crucified;
In memory of My dying love
  Do this, He said, and died.

2   The badge and token this,
    The sure confirming seal
That He is ours, and we are His,
  The servants of His will:
  His dear peculiar ones,
  The purchase of His Blood;
His Blood which once for all atones,
  And brings us *now* to GOD.

3   Then let us still profess
    Our Master's honour'd name,
Stand forth His faithful witnesses,
  True followers of the Lamb:

In proof that such we are
His saying we receive,
And thus to all mankind declare
We *do* in CHRIST believe.

4   Part of His Church below,
We thus our right maintain;
Our living membership we show,
And in the fold remain.
The sheep of *Israel's* fold
In *England's* pastures fed,
And fellowship with all we hold
Who hold it with our Head.

HYMN XIV.

1 FATHER, hear the Blood of JESUS,
Speaking in Thine ears above!
From Thy wrath and curse release us,
Manifest Thy pardoning love.
O receive us to Thy favour,
For His only sake receive;
Give us to our bleeding Saviour;
Let us by Thy dying live.

2 " To Thy pardoning grace receive them,"
Once He pray'd upon the tree;
Still His Blood cries out, " Forgive them,
All their sins were purg'd by Me."

3 Still our Advocate in heaven
  Prays the prayer on earth begun,
"Father, show their sins forgiven,
  Father, glorify Thy Son!"

HYMN XV.

1 DYING Friend of sinners, hear us,
  Humbly at Thy Cross who lie,
In Thine Ordinance be near us,
  Now the ungodly justify;
Let Thy bowels of compassion
  To Thy ransom'd creatures move,
Show us all Thy great salvation,
  GOD of truth and GOD of love.

2 By Thy meritorious dying
  Save us from the death of sin,
By Thy precious Blood's applying
  Make our inmost nature clean;
Give us worthily to adore Thee,
  Thou our full Redeemer be:
Give us pardon, grace, and glory,
  Peace, and power, and heaven in Thee.

HYMN XVI.

1 COME, Thou everlasting Spirit,
    Bring to every thankful mind
All the Saviour's dying merit,
    All His sufferings for mankind;
True Recorder of His Passion,
    Now the living faith impart,
Now reveal His great salvation,
    Preach His Gospel to our heart.

2 Come, Thou witness of His dying,
    Come, remembrancer Divine,
Let us feel Thy power applying
    CHRIST to every soul and mine;
Let us groan Thine inward groaning,
    Look on Him we pierc'd, and grieve;
All receive the grace-atoning,
    All the sprinkled Blood receive,

HYMN XVII.

1 WHO is this that comes from far
    Clad in garments dipped in blood!
Strong triumphant traveller,
Is He man, or is He GOD?

2 I that speak in righteousness,
   Son of God and Man I am,
   Mighty to redeem your race;
   Jesus is your Saviour's name.

3 Wherefore are Thy garments red,
   Dyed as in a crimson sea?
   They that in the wine-fat tread
   Are not stain'd so much as Thee.

4 I, the Father's favourite Son,
   Have the dreadful wine-press trod,
   Borne the vengeful wrath alone,
   All the fiercest wrath of God.

HYMN XVIII.

1 LIFT your eyes of faith, and look
      On the signs He did ordain!
   Thus the Bread of Life was broke,
   Thus the Lamb of God was slain,
   Thus was shed on *Calvary*
   His last drop of Blood for me!

2 See the slaughter'd Sacrifice,
   See the Altar stain'd with Blood!
   Crucified before our eyes,
   Faith discerns the dying God;
   Dying that our souls might live,
   Gasping at His death, Forgive!

HYMN XIX.

1 FORGIVE, the Saviour cries,
     They know not what they do :
Forgive, my heart replies,
     And all my soul renew ;
I claim the kingdom in Thy right,
     Who now Thy sufferings share,
And mount with Thee to *Zion's* height,
     And see Thy glory there.

HYMN XX.

1 LAMB of God, whose bleeding love
     We thus recall to mind,
Send the answer from above,
     And let us mercy find ;
Think on us, who think on Thee,
And every struggling soul release :
     O remember *Calvary,*
     And bid us go in peace.

2 By Thine agonizing pain
     And bloody sweat we pray,
By Thy dying love to man,
     Take all our sins away ;

Burst our bonds, and set us free,
From all iniquity release:
   O remember *Calvary*,
     And bid us go in peace.

3   Let Thy Blood by faith applied,
     The sinner's pardon seal,
Speak us freely justified,
     And all our sickness heal:
By Thy Passion on the tree
Let all our griefs and troubles cease:
   O remember *Calvary*,
     And bid us go in peace.

4   Never will we hence depart,
     Till Thou our wants relieve,
Write forgiveness on our heart,
     And all Thine image give:
Still our souls shall cry to Thee
Till perfected in holiness:
   O remember *Calvary*,
     And bid us go in peace.

HYMN XXI.

1 GOD of unexampled grace,
     Redeemer of mankind,
Matter of eternal praise
     We in Thy Passion find:

Still our choicest strains we bring,
Still the joyful theme pursue,
Thee the Friend of sinners sing,
Whose love is ever new.

2 Endless scenes of wonder rise
    With that mysterious Tree,
Crucified before our eyes,
    Where we our Maker see:
Jesus, Lord, what hast Thou done?
Publish we the death divine,
Stop, and gaze, and fall, and own
    Was never love like Thine!

3 Never love nor sorrow was
    Like that my Jesus shew'd;
See Him stretch'd on yonder Cross,
    And crush'd beneath our load!
Now discern the Deity,
Now His heavenly birth declare;
Faith cries out, 'Tis He! 'tis He!
    My God, that suffers there.

4 Jesus drinks the bitter cup,
    The wine-press treads alone,
Tears the graves and mountains up
    By His expiring groan.
Lo! the powers of heaven He shakes;
Nature in convulsions lies;
Earth's profoundest centre quakes:
    The great Jehovah dies!

5 Dies the glorious Cause of all,
   The true eternal *Pan*,
Falls to raise us from our fall,
   To ransom sinful man :
Well may *Sol* withdraw his light,
With the Sufferer sympathise,
Leave the world in sudden night,
   While his Creator dies.

6 Well may heaven be cloth'd with black,
   And solemn sackcloth wear,
JESU's agony partake,
   The hour of darkness share :
Mourn the astonied hosts above,
Silence saddens all the skies ;
Kindler of seraphic love,
   The GOD of angels dies.

7 Oh, my GOD, He dies for me,
   I feel the mortal smart !
See Him hanging on the tree,—
   A sight that breaks my heart !
O that all to Thee might turn !
Sinners, ye may love Him too,
Look on Him ye pierc'd, and mourn
   For one who bled for you.

8 Weep o'er your Desire and Hope
   With tears of humblest love ;
Sing, for JESUS is gone up,
   And reigns enthron'd above !

Lives our Head, to die no more:
Power is all to JESUS given,
Worshipp'd as He was before,
    The immortal King of heaven.

9 LORD, we bless Thee for Thy grace
    And truth which never fail,
Hastening to behold Thy face
    Without a dimming veil:
We shall see our heavenly King,
All Thy glorious love proclaim,
Help the angel choirs to sing
    Our dear triumphant Lamb.

HYMN XXII.

1 PRINCE of Life for sinners slain,
    Grant us fellowship with Thee;
Fain we would partake Thy pain,
Share Thy mortal agony;
Give us now the dreadful power,
Now bring back Thy dying hour.

2 Place us near the accursed wood
Where Thou didst Thy life resign,
Near as once Thy mother stood;
Partners of the pangs divine,
Bid us feel her sacred smart,
Feel the sword that pierc'd her heart.

3 Surely now the prayer He hears:
　Faith presents the Crucified!
　Lo! the wounded Lamb appears!
　Pierc'd His feet, His hands, His side,
　Hangs our hope on yonder Tree,
　Hangs and bleeds to death for me!

HYMN XXIII.

1 HEARTS of stone, relent, relent,
　　Break by Jesu's Cross subdued;
　See His Body mangled, rent,
　Cover'd with a gore of blood!
　Sinful soul, what hast thou done?
　Murder'd God's eternal Son!

2 Yes, our sins have done the deed,
　Drove the nails that fix Him here,
　Crown'd with thorns His sacred head,
　Pierced Him with a soldier's spear,
　Made His soul a Sacrifice;
　For a sinful world He dies.

3 Shall we let Him die in vain?
　Still to death pursue our God?
　Open tear His Wounds again,
　Trample on His precious Blood?
　No; with all our sins we part:
　Saviour, take my broken heart!

HYMN XXIV.

1 EXPIRING in the sinner's place,
   Crushed with the universal load,
He hangs!—adown His mournful face,
See trickling fast the tears and blood!
The Blood that purges all our stains,
It starts in rivers from His veins.

2 A fountain gushes from His side,
Opened that all may enter in,
That all may feel the death applied,
The death of GOD, the death of sin,
The death by which our foes are killed,
The death by which our souls are healed.

HYMN XXV.

1 IN an accepted time of love
   To Thee, O JESUS, we draw near;
Wilt Thou not the veil remove,
And meet Thy mournful followers here,
Who humbly at Thy Altar lie,
And wait to find Thee passing by?

2 Thou bidd'st us call Thy death to mind,
And Thou must give the solemn power:
Come then, Thou Saviour of mankind,
Bring back that last tremendous hour,
And stand in all Thy Wounds confest,
And wrap us in Thy bloody vest.

3 With reverential faith we claim
　Our share in Thy great Sacrifice :
　Come, O Thou all-atoning Lamb,
　Revive us by Thy dying cries ;
　Apply to all Thy healing Blood,
　And sprinkle *me, my* LORD, *my* GOD !

HYMN XXVI.

1 'TIS done ! the atoning work is done :
　　JESUS, the world's Redeemer, dies !
　All nature feels the important groan
　Loud echoing through the earth and skies ;
　The earth doth to her centre quake,
　And heaven as hell's deep gloom is black !

2 The temple's veil is rent in twain,
　While JESUS meekly bows His head,
　The rocks resent His mortal pain,
　The yawning graves give up their dead,
　The bodies of the saints arise,
　Reviving as their Saviour dies.

3 And shall not we His death partake,
　In sympathetic anguish groan ?
　O Saviour, let Thy Passion shake
　Our earth, and rend our hearts of stone,
　To second life our souls restore,
　And wake us that we sleep no more.

HYMN XXVII.

1 ROCK of *Israel*, cleft for me,
    For us, for all mankind,
See Thy feeblest followers, see,
    Who call Thy death to mind :
Sion is the very land ;
Us beneath Thy shade receive,
Grant us in the cleft to stand,
    And by Thy death to live.

2 In this howling wilderness,
    On *Calvary's* steep top,
Made a curse our souls to bless,
    Thou once wast lifted up ;
Stricken there by *Moses'* rod,
Wounded with a deadly blow,
Gushing streams of life o'erflow'd
    The thirsty world below.

3 Rivers of salvation still
    Along the desert roll,
Rivers to refresh and heal
    The fainting sin-sick soul ;
Still the fountain of Thy Blood
Stands for sinners open'd wide,
Now, e'en now, my Lord and God,
    I wash me in Thy side.

4 Now, e'en now, we all plunge in,
    And drink the purple wave,
This the antidote of sin,
    'Tis this our souls shall save :
With the life of JESUS fed,
Lo ! from strength to strength we rise,
Follow'd by our Rock, and led
    To meet Him in the skies.

HYMN XXVIII.

1

UTHOR of our salvation, Thee
With lowly thankful hearts we praise,
Author of this great Mystery,
Figure and means of saving grace.

2 The sacred true effectual sign
   Thy Body and Thy Blood it shews,
   The glorious instrument divine
   Thy mercy and Thy strength bestows.

3 We see the Blood that seals our peace,
   Thy pardoning mercy we receive :
   The bread doth visibly express
   The strength through which our spirits live.

4 Our spirits drink a fresh supply,
   And eat the Bread so freely given,
   Till borne on eagle's wings we fly,
   And banquet with our LORD in heaven.

HYMN XXIX.

1 O THOU who this mysterious Bread
    Didst in *Emmaus* break,
Return herewith our souls to feed,
    And to Thy followers speak.

2 Unseal the volume of Thy grace,
    Apply the gospel word,
Open our eyes to see Thy face,
    Our hearts to know the LORD.

3 Of Thee we commune still, and mourn
    Till Thou the veil remove;
Talk with us, and our hearts shall burn
    With flames of fervent love.

4 Enkindle now the heavenly zeal,
    And make Thy mercy known,
And give our pardon'd souls to feel
    That GOD and love are one.

HYMN XXX.

1 JESU, at whose supreme command
    We thus approach to GOD,
Before us in Thy vesture stand,
    Thy vesture dipt in blood.

2 Obedient to Thy gracious word
     We break the hallowed Bread,
Commemorate Thee, our dying LORD,
     And trust on Thee to feed.

3 Now, Saviour, now Thyself reveal,
     And make Thy nature known,
Affix the Sacramental seal,
     And stamp us for Thine own.

4 The tokens of Thy dying love,
     O let us all receive,
And feel the quickening Spirit move,
     And *sensibly* believe.

5 The Cup of Blessing blest by Thee,
     Let it Thy Blood impart ;
The Bread Thy mystic Body be,
     And cheer each languid heart.

6 The grace which sure salvation brings,
     Let us herewith receive ;
Satiate the hungry with good things,
     The hidden Manna give.

7 The living Bread sent down from heaven
     In us vouchsafe to be ;
Thy Flesh for all the world is given,
     And all may live by Thee.

8 Now, LORD, on us Thy Flesh bestow,
   And let us drink Thy Blood,
 Till all our souls are filled below
   With all the life of GOD.

HYMN XXXI.

1 O ROCK of our salvation, see
   The souls that seek their rest in Thee;
 Beneath Thy cooling shadow hide,
 And keep us, Saviour, in Thy side;
 By Water and by Blood redeem,
 And wash us in the mingled stream.

2 The sin-atoning Blood apply,
 And let the Water sanctify;
 Pardon and holiness impart,
 Sprinkle and purify our heart;
 Wash out the last remains of sin,
 And make our inmost nature clean.

3 The double stream in pardon rolls,
 And brings Thy love into our souls:
 Who dare the truth divine receive,
 And credence to Thy witness give,
 We here Thy utmost power shall prove,
 Thy utmost power of perfect love.

HYMN XXXII.

1 JESU, to Thee for help we call,
    Plunged in the depth of *Adam's* fall,
      Plagued with a carnal heart and mind;
No distance, or of time or place,
Secures us from the foul disgrace
      By him entail'd on all mankind.

2 Six thousand years are now pass'd by,
    Yet still like him we sin and die,
      As born within his house we were;
As each were that accursed *Cain*,
We feel the all-polluting stain,
      And groan our inbred sin to bear.

3 Thou GOD of sanctifying love,
    Adam descended from above,
      The virtue of Thy Blood impart;
O let it reach to all below,
As far extend, as freely flow,
      To cleanse, as his to infect, our heart.

4 Ruin in him complete we have,
    And canst not Thou as greatly save,
      And fully here our loss repair?
Thou canst, Thou wilt, we dare believe,
We here Thy nature shall retrieve,
      And all Thy heavenly image bear.

HYMN XXXIII.

1 JESU, dear redeeming LORD,
　　Magnify Thy dying word;
In Thy Ordinance appear,
Come and meet Thy followers here.

2 In the Rite Thou hast enjoin'd,
　Let us now our Saviour find;
Drink Thy Blood for sinners shed,
Taste Thee in the broken Bread.

3 Thou our faithful hearts prepare,
　Thou Thy pardoning grace declare;
Thou that hast for sinners died,
Show Thyself the Crucified!

4 All the power of sin remove,
　Fill us with Thy perfect love,
Stamp us with the stamp divine,
Seal our souls for ever Thine.

HYMN XXXIV.

1 LORD of Life, Thy followers see,
　　Hungering, thirsting after Thee,
At Thy sacred Table feed,
Nourish us with Living Bread.

2 Cheer us with immortal Wine,
Heavenly sustenance divine,
Grant us now a fresh supply,
Now relieve us, or we die.

HYMN XXXV.

1 O THOU Paschal Lamb of God,
　　Feed us with Thy Flesh and Blood;
Life and strength Thy death supplies,
Feast us on Thy Sacrifice.

2 Quicken our dead souls again,
Then our living souls sustain,
Then in us Thy life keep up,
Then confirm our faith and hope.

3 Still, O Lord, our strength repair,
Till renew'd in love we are,
Till Thy utmost grace we prove,
All Thy life of perfect love.

HYMN XXXVI.

1 AMAZING mystery of love!
　　While posting to eternal pain,
God saw His rebels from above,
And stoop'd into a mortal man.

2 His mercy cast a pitying look ;
By love, mere causeless love, inclined,
Our guilt and punishment He took,
And died a victim for mankind.

3 His Blood procur'd our life and peace,
And quench'd the wrath of hostile heaven;
Justice gave way to our release,
And God hath all *my* sins forgiven.

4 Jesu, our pardon we receive,
The purchase of that Blood of Thine,
And now begin by grace to live,
And breathe the breath of love divine.

HYMN XXXVII.

1 BUT soon the tender life will die,
Though bought by Thy atoning Blood,
Unless Thou grant a fresh supply,
And wash us in the watery flood.

2 The Blood remov'd our guilt in vain,
If sin in us must always stay ;
But Thou shalt purge our inbred stain,
And wash its relics all away.

3 The stream that from Thy wounded side
In blended Blood and Water flow'd,
Shall cleanse whom first it justified,
And fill us with the life of God.

4 Proceeds from Thee the double grace ;
  Two effluxes with life divine,
  To quicken all the faithful race,
  In one eternal current join.

5 Saviour, Thou didst not come from heaven
  By Water or by Blood alone ;
  Thou diedst that we might live forgiven,
  And all be sanctified in one.

HYMN XXXVIII.

1 WORTHY the Lamb of endless praise,
      Whose double life we here shall prove,
  The pardoning and the hallowing grace,
  The childish and the perfect love.

2 We here shall gain our calling's prize,
  The Gift Unspeakable receive,
  And higher still in death arise,
  And all the life of glory live.

3 To make our right and title sure,
  Our dying Lord Himself hath given ;
  His Sacrifice did all procure,
  Pardon, and holiness, and heaven.

4 Our life of grace we here shall feel,
  Shed in our loving hearts abroad,

Till CHRIST our glorious life reveal,
Long hidden with Himself in GOD.

5 Come, dear Redeemer of mankind,
We long Thy open face to see ;
Appear, and all who seek shall find
Their bliss consummated in Thee.

6 Thy Presence shall the cloud dispart,
Thy Presence shall the life display;
Then, then our all in all Thou art,
Our fulness of eternal day.

HYMN XXXIX.

1 SINNERS, with awe draw near,
And find thy SAVIOUR here,
In His Ordinances still ;
Touch His Sacramental clothes,
Present in His power to heal,
Virtue from His Body flows.

2 His Body is the seat
Where all our blessings meet,
Full of unexhausted worth;
Still it makes the sinner whole,
Pours divine effusions forth,
Life to every dying soul.

3   Pardon, and power, and peace,
      And perfect righteousness
From that sacred Fountain springs ;
Wash'd in His all-cleansing Blood,
Rise, ye worms, to priests and kings,
Rise in CHRIST, and reign with GOD.

HYMN XL.

1   AUTHOR of life divine,
      Who hast a Table spread,
Furnish'd with mystic Wine
And everlasting Bread,
Preserve the life Thyself hast given,
And feed, and train us up for heaven.

2   Our needy souls sustain
      With fresh supplies of love,
Till all Thy life we gain,
And all Thy fulness prove ;
And strengthen'd by Thy perfect grace,
Behold without a veil Thy face.

HYMN XLI.

1   TRUTH of the Paschal Sacrifice,
      JESU, regard Thy people's cries,
Nor let us in our sins remain ;

Surely Thou hear'st the prisoners groan,
Come down to our relief, come down,
   And break the dire accuser's chain.

2 Humble the proud oppressive king,
Deliverance to Thine *Israel* bring ;
   And while the unsprinkled victims die,
Thy death for us present to God,
Write our protection in Thy Blood,
   And bid the hellish fiend pass by.

HYMN XLII.

1 GLORY to Him who freely spent
   His Blood that we might live,
And through this choicest instrument
   Doth all His blessings give.

2 Fasting He doth, and hearing bless
   And prayer can much avail,
Good vessels all to draw the grace
   Out of salvation's well.

3 But none like this mysterious Rite
   Which dying mercy gave,
Can draw forth all His promis'd might
   And all His will to save.

4 This is the richest legacy
    Thou hast on man bestow'd ;
Here chiefly, LORD, we feed on Thee,
    And drink Thy precious Blood.

5 Here all Thy blessings we receive,
    Here all Thy gifts are given ;
To those that would in Thee believe,
    Pardon, and grace, and heaven.

6 Thus may we still in Thee be blest
    Till all from earth remove,
And share with Thee the marriage feast,
    And drink the wine above.

HYMN XLIII.

1   SAVIOUR, and can it be
     That Thou shouldst dwell with me ?
From Thy high and lofty throne,
Throne of everlasting bliss,
Will Thy Majesty stoop down
To so mean a house as this ?

2   I am not worthy, LORD,
     So foul, so self-abhorr'd,
Thee, my GOD, to entertain
In this poor polluted heart ;
I am a frail sinful man,
All my nature cries, Depart !

3   Yet come, Thou heavenly Guest,
         And purify my breast;
Come, Thou great and glorious King,
While before Thy Cross I bow;
With Thyself salvation bring,
Cleanse the house by entering now.

HYMN XLIV.

1 OUR Passover for us is slain,
      The tokens of His death remain, .
   On these authentic signs imprest:
By JESUS out of *Egypt* led,
Still on the paschal Lamb we feed,
      And keep the Sacramental Feast.

2 That arm that smote the parting sea
   Is still stretch'd out for us, for me:
      The angel GOD is still our guide,
And lest we in the desert faint,
We find our spirits' every want
      By constant miracle supplied.

3 Thy Flesh for our support is given,
   Thou art the Bread sent down from heaven,
      That all mankind by Thee might live;
O that we evermore may prove
The manna of Thy quickening love,
      And all Thy life of grace receive!

4 Nourish us to that awful day
  When types and veils shall pass away,
    And perfect grace in glory end;
  Us for the marriage feast prepare,
  Unfurl Thy banner in the air,
    And bid Thy saints to heaven ascend.

HYMN XLV.

1 TREMENDOUS love to lost mankind!
    Could none but CHRIST the ransom find?
    Could none but CHRIST the pardon buy?
  How great the sin of *Adam's* race!
  How greater still the Saviour's grace,
    When GOD doth for His creature die!

2 Not heaven so rich a grace can shew
  As this He did on worms bestow,
    Those darlings of the Incarnate GOD;
  Less favour'd were the angel powers;
  Their crowns are cheaper far than ours,
    Nor ever cost the Lamb His Blood.

3 Our souls eternally to save,
  More than ten thousand worlds He gave;
    That we might know our sins forgiven,
  That we might in Thy glory shine,
  The purchase price was Blood Divine,
    And bought the Aceldema of heaven.

4 JESU, we bless Thy saving Name,
   And trusting in Thy merits claim
      Our rich inheritance above;
   Thou shalt Thy ransom'd servants own,
   And raise and seat us on Thy throne,
      Dear objects of Thy dying love.

HYMN XLVI.

1 HOW richly is the Table stor'd
      Of JESUS our redeeming LORD!
   Melchisedec and *Aaron* join
   To furnish out the Feast Divine.

2 *Aaron* for us the Blood hath shed,
   Melchisedec bestows the Bread,
   To nourish this, and that to atone;
   And both the priests in CHRIST are one.

3 JESUS appears to sacrifice,
   The Flesh and Blood Himself supplies;
   Enter'd the veil, His death He pleads,
   And blesses all our souls, and feeds.

4 'Tis here He meets the faithful line,
   Sustains us with His Bread and Wine;
   We feel the double grace is given,
   And gladly urge our way to heaven.

HYMN XLVII.

1 JESU, Thy weakest servants bless,
　　Give what these hallow'd signs express.
　And what Thou giv'st secure ;
Pardon into my soul convey,
Strength in Thy pardoning love to stay,
　And to the end endure.

2 Raise, and enable me to stand,
　Save out of the destroyer's hand
　　This helpless soul of mine ;
Vouchsafe me then Thy strengthening grace,
And with the arms of love embrace,
　And keep me ever Thine.

HYMN XLVIII.

1 SAVIOUR of my soul from sin,
　　Thou my kind preserver be,
　Stablish what Thou dost begin,
　Carry on Thy work in me,
　All Thy faithful mercies shew,
　Hold, and never let me go.

2 Never let me lose my peace,
　Forfeit what Thy goodness gave,
　Give it still, and still increase,
　Save me, and persist to save,
　Seal the grant conferr'd before,
　Give Thy blessing evermore.

HYMN XLIX.

1 SON of GOD, Thy blessing grant,
  Still supply my every want,
Tree of Life, Thine influence shed,
With Thy sap my spirit feed.

2 Tenderest branch, alas, am I,
Wither without Thee and die,
Weak as helpless infancy,
O confirm my soul in Thee.

3 Unsustained by Thee I fall;
Send the strength for which I call:
Weaker than a bruised reed,
Help I every moment need.

4 All my hopes on Thee depend;
Love me, save me to the end,
Give me the continuing grace,
Take the everlasting praise.

HYMN L.

1 FATHER of everlasting love,
  Whose bowels of compassion move
  To all Thy gracious hands have made,
See, in the howling desert see
A soul from *Egypt* brought by Thee,
  And help me with Thy constant aid.

2 Ah, do not, LORD, Thine own forsake,
Nor let my feeble soul look back,
  Or basely turn to sin again,
No, never let me faint or tire,
But travel on in strong desire,
  Till I my heavenly *Canaan* gain.

HYMN LI.

1 THOU very Paschal Lamb,
    Whose Blood for us was shed,
Through Whom we out of *Egypt* came;
  Thy ransom'd people lead.

2   Angel of Gospel-grace,
    Fulfil Thy character;
To guard and feed the chosen race,
  In *Israel's* camp appear.

3   Throughout the desert way
    Conduct us by Thy light;
Be Thou a cooling cloud by day,
  A cheering fire by night.

4   Our fainting souls sustain
    With blessings from above,
And ever on Thy people rain
  The manna of Thy love.

HYMN LII.

1 O THOU, who hanging on the Cross
　　Didst buy our pardon with Thy Blood,
Canst Thou not still maintain our cause,
And fill us with the Life of God,
Bless with the blessings of Thy throne,
And perfect all our souls in one?

2 Lo! on Thy bloody Sacrifice
For all our graces we depend;
Supported by Thy Cross arise,
To finish'd holiness ascend,
And gain on earth the mountain's height,
And then salute our friends in light.

HYMN LIII.

1 O GOD of truth and love,
　　Let us Thy mercy prove,
Bless Thine Ordinance divine,
Let it now effectual be,
Answer all its great design,—
All its gracious ends in me.

E

2   O might the sacred Word
      Set forth our dying LORD,
Point us to Thy sufferings past,
Present grace and strength impart,
Give our ravish'd souls a taste,
Pledge of glory in our heart.

3   Come in Thy Spirit down,
      Thine Institution crown:
LAMB of GOD, as slain appear,
Life of all believers Thou,
Let us now perceive Thee near,
Come, Thou Hope of glory, now.

HYMN LIV.

1 WHY did my dying LORD ordain
      This dear Memorial of His love?
Might we not all by faith obtain,
By faith the mountain sin remove,
Enjoy the sense of sins forgiven,
And holiness, the taste of heaven?

2 It seem'd to my Redeemer good
That faith should *here* His coming wait,
Should here receive Immortal Food,—
Grow up in Him divinely great,
And fill'd with holy violence seize
The glorious crown of righteousness.

3 Saviour, Thou didst this Mystery give,
  That I Thy nature might partake;
  Thou bidd'st me outward signs receive,
  One with Thyself my soul to make;
  My body, soul, and spirit join
  Inseparably one with Thine.

4 The prayer, the fast, the Word, conveys,
  When mix'd with faith, Thy life to me;
  In all the channels of Thy grace
  I still have fellowship with Thee,
  But chiefly here my soul is fed
  With fulness of Immortal Bread.

5 Communion closer far I feel,
  And deeper drink the atoning Blood;
  The joy is more unspeakable,
  And yields me larger draughts of GOD,
  Till nature faints beneath the power,
  And faith filled up can hold no more.

HYMN LV.

1 'TIS not a dead, external sign
    Which here my hopes require;
  The living power of love divine
    In JESUS I desire.

2 I want the dear Redeemer's grace,
   I seek the Crucified,
The Man that suffer'd in my place,
   The God that groan'd and died.

3 Swift as their rising Lord to find,
   The two disciples ran,
I seek the Saviour of mankind,
   Nor shall I seek in vain.

4 Come, all who long His face to see
   That did our burden bear,
Hasten to *Calvary* with me,
   And we shall find Him there.

HYMN LVI.

1 HOW dreadful is the Mystery,
   Which, instituted, Lord, by Thee,
   Or life or death conveys!
Death to the impious and profane;
Nor shall our faith in Thee be vain,
   Who here expect Thy grace.

2 Who eats unworthily this Bread
Pulls down Thy curses on his head,
   And eats his deadly bane;

And shall not we who rightly eat
Live by the salutary Meat,
  And equal blessings gain?

3 Destruction, if Thy Body shed,
And strike the soul of sinners dead,
  Who dare the signs abuse;
Surely the instrument divine,
To all that are or would be Thine,
  Shall saving health diffuse.

4 Saviour of life, and joy, and bliss,
Pardon, and power, and perfect peace
  We shall herewith receive;
The grace implied through faith is given,
And we that eat the Bread of heaven
  The life of heaven shall live.

HYMN LVII.

1 O THE depth of love Divine,
  The unfathomable grace!
Who shall say how Bread and Wine
  God into man conveys,
How the Bread His Flesh imparts,
How the Wine transmits His Blood,
Fills His faithful people's hearts
  With all the life of God?

2 Let the wisest mortal shew
 How we the grace receive:
Feeble elements bestow
 A power not theirs to give:
Who explains the wondrous way?
How thro' these the virtue came?
These the virtue did convey,
 Yet still remain the same.

3 How can heavenly spirits rise,
 By earthly matter fed,
Drink herewith Divine supplies,
 And eat Immortal Bread?
Ask the Father's wisdom *how*,
Him that did the means ordain;
Angels round our Altars bow
 To search it out in vain.

4 Sure and real is the grace,
 The manner be unknown;
Only meet us in Thy ways,
 And perfect us in one.
Let us taste the heavenly powers;
Lord, we ask for nothing more:
Thine to bless, 'tis only ours
 To wonder and adore.

HYMN LVIII.

1 HOW long, Thou faithful God, shall I
    Here in Thy ways forgotten lie?
When shall the means of healing be
The channels of Thy grace to me?

2 Sinners on every side step in,
And wash away their pain and sin;
But I, a helpless, sin-sick soul,
Still lie expiring at the pool.

3 In vain I take the broken Bread;
I cannot on Thy mercy feed:
In vain I drink the hallow'd Wine;
I cannot taste the love Divine.

4 Angel and Son of God, come down,
Thy Sacramental Banquet crown;
Thy power into the means infuse,
And give them now their sacred use.

5 Thou seest me lying at the pool;
I would, Thou know'st I would, be whole:
O let the troubled waters move,
And minister Thy healing love.

6 Break to me now the hallow'd Bread,
And bid me on Thy Body feed;
Give me the Wine, Almighty God,
And let me drink Thy precious Blood.

7 Surely, if Thou the symbols bless,
The Covenant Blood shall seal my peace ;
The Flesh e'en now shall be my food,
And all my soul be fill'd with GOD.

HYMN LIX.

1 GOD incomprehensible,
　　Shall man presume to know,
Fully search Him out, or tell
　　His wondrous ways below ?
Him in all His ways we find ;
How the means transmit the power,
Here He leaves our thoughts behind,
　　And faith inquires no more.

2 How He did these creatures raise,
　　And make this Bread and Wine
Organs to convey His grace
　　To this poor soul of mine,
I cannot the way descry,
Need not know the mystery :
Only this I know, that I
　　Was blind, but now I see.

3 Now mine eyes are open'd wide
　　To see His pardoning love,
Here I view the God that died
　　My ruin to remove.

Clay upon mine eyes He laid
(I at once my sight receiv'd),
Bless'd and bid me eat the Bread,
And, lo! my soul believ'd.

HYMN LX.

1 COME to the Feast; for CHRIST invites,
　　And promises to feed;
'Tis here His closest love invites
　　The members to their Head.

2 'Tis here He nourishes His own
　　With living Bread from heaven,
Or makes Himself to mourners known,
　　And shows their sins forgiven.

3 Still in His instituted ways
　　He bids us ask the power,
The pardoning or the hallowing grace,
　　And wait the appointed hour.

4 'Tis not for us to set our GOD
　　A time His grace to give;
The benefit whene'er bestow'd,
　　We gladly should receive.

5 Who seek redemption thro' His love,
   His love shall them redeem ;
He came self-emptied from above,
   That we might live thro' Him.

6 Expect we then the quickening word,
   Who at His Altar bow.
But if it be Thy pleasure, LORD,
   O let us find Thee now !

HYMN LXI.

1 THOU GOD of boundless power and grace,
   How wonderful are all Thy ways !
How far above our loftiest thought !
In presence of the meanest things
(While all from Thee the virtue springs)
   Thy most stupendous works are wrought.

2 Struck by a stroke of *Moses'* rod,
The parting sea confess'd its GOD,
   And high in crystal bulwarks rose ;
At *Moses'* beck it burst the chain,
Return'd to all its strength again,
   And swept to hell Thy Church's foes.

3 Let but Thy ark the walls surround,
Let but the ram's-horn trumpet sound,
　　The city boasts its height no more;
Its bulwarks are at once o'erthrown,
Its massy walls by air blown down;
　　They fall before Almighty power.

4 *Jordan* at Thy command shall heal
The sore disease incurable,
　　And wash out all the leper's stains;
Or oil the medicine shall supply,
Or clothes, or shadows passing by,
　　If so Thy sovereign will ordains:

5 Yet not from these the power proceeds,
Trumpets, or rods, or clothes, or shades;
　　Thy only arm the work hath done.
If instruments Thy wisdom choose,
Thy grace confers their saving use;
　　Salvation is from GOD alone.

6 Thou in this Sacramental Bread
Dost now our hungry spirits feed,
　　And cheer us with the hallow'd Wine
(Communion of Thy Flesh and Blood).
We banquet on Immortal Food,
　　And drink the Stream of Life Divine.

HYMN LXII.

1 THE heavenly ordinances shine,
   And speak their origin Divine ;
The stars diffuse their golden blaze,
And glitter to their Maker's praise.

2 They each in different glory bright,
With stronger or with feebler light,
Their influence on mortals shed,
And cheer us by their friendly aid.

3 The Gospel ordinances here
As stars in JESU's Church appear ;
His power they more or less declare,
But all His heavenly impress bear.

4 Around our lower orb they burn,
And cheer and bless us in their turn,
Transmit the light by JESU given,
The faithful witnesses of heaven.

5 They steer the pilgrim's course aright,
And, bounteous of their borrow'd light,
Conduct throughout the desert way,
And lead us to eternal day.

6 But, first of the celestial train,
Benignest to the sons of men,
The *Sacramental Glory* shines,
And answers all our GOD's designs.

7 The Heavenly Host it passes far,
  Illustrious as the Morning Star,
  The Light of Life Divine imparts,
  While JESUS rises in our hearts.

8 With joy we feel its sacred power,
  But neither stars nor means adore;
  We take the blessing from above,
  And praise the GOD of Truth and Love.

9 What He did for our use ordain
  Shall still from age to age remain;
  Whoe'er rejects the kind command,
  The Word of GOD shall ever stand.

10 Go, foolish worms, His Word deny;
  Go, tear those planets from the sky;
  But while the sun and moon endure,
  The Ordinance on earth is sure.

HYMN LXIII.

1 O GOD, Thy Word we claim;
  Thou here record'st Thy Name.
  Visit us in pardoning grace;
  CHRIST the Crucified appear:
  Come in Thy appointed ways;
  Come, and meet, and bless us here.

2   No local deity
     We worship, LORD, in Thee:
Free Thy grace, and unconfin'd,
Yet it here doth freest move.
In the means Thy love enjoin'd
Look we for Thy richest love.

HYMN LXIV.

1   O THE grace on man bestow'd!
     Here my dearest LORD I see
Offering up His Death to GOD,
Giving all His Life to me.
GOD for JESU's sake forgives;
Man by JESU's Spirit lives.

2   Yes, Thy Sacrament extends
All the blessings of Thy Death
To the soul that here attends,
Longs to feel Thy quickening breath;
Surely we who wait shall prove
All Thy life of perfect love.

HYMN LXV.

1 BLEST be the LORD, for ever blest,
   Who bought us with a price,
And bids His ransom'd servants feast
   On His great Sacrifice.

2 Thy Blood was shed upon the Cross
   To wash us white as snow;
Broken for us Thy Body was
   To feed our souls below.

3 Now, on the Sacred Table laid,
   Thy Flesh becomes our food;
Thy Life is to our souls convey'd
   In Sacramental Blood.

4 We eat the Offering of our peace,
   The hidden Manna prove,
And only live to adore and bless
   Thine all-sufficient love.

HYMN LXVI.

1 JESU, my LORD and GOD, bestow
   All which Thy Sacrament doth shew,
   And make the real sign

A sure effectual means of grace,
Then sanctify my heart, and bless,
And make it all like Thine.

2 Great is Thy faithfulness and love ;
Thine Ordinance can never prove
Of none effect and vain ;
Only do Thou my heart prepare,
And find Thy Real Presence there,
And all Thy fulness gain.

HYMN LXVII.

1 FATHER, I offer Thee Thine own,
This worthless soul, and Thou Thy Son
Dost offer here to me :
Wilt Thou so mean a gift receive,
And will the holy JESUS live
With loathsome leprosy ?

2 Saint of the LORD, my soul is sin,
Yet, O eternal Priest, come in,
And cleanse Thy mean abode,
Convert into a sacred shrine,
And count this abject soul of mine
A temple meet for GOD.

HYMN LXVIII.

1   JESU, Son of GOD, draw near,
     Hasten to my sepulchre;
Help, where dead in sin I lie;
Save, or I for ever die.

2   Let no savour of the grave
Stop Thy power to help and save;
Call me forth to life restor'd,
Quicken'd by my dying LORD.

3   By Thine all-atoning Blood
Raise and bring me now to GOD,
Now pronounce my sins forgiven,
Loose, and let me go to heaven.

HYMN LXIX.

1   SINFUL, and blind, and poor,
     And lost without Thy grace,
Thy mercy I implore,
     And wait to see Thy face.
Begging I sit by the wayside,
And long to know the Crucified.

2   Jesu, attend my cry,
Thou Son of *David*, hear;
If now Thou passest by,
Stand still and call me near:
The darkness from my heart remove,
And shew me now Thy pardoning love.

HYMN LXX.

Happy the man to whom 'tis given
  To eat the Bread of Life in heaven:
This happiness in Christ we prove,
Who feed on His forgiving love.

HYMN LXXI.

1 Draw near, ye blood-besprinkled race,
    And take what God vouchsafes to give;
The outward sign of inward grace,
Ordain'd by Christ Himself, receive:
The sign transmits the Signified,
The grace is by the means applied.

2 Sure pledges of His dying love,
Receive the Sacramental Meat,

And feel the virtue from above ;
The mystic Flesh of JESUS eat,
Drink with the wine His healing Blood,
And feast on the Incarnate GOD.

3 Gross misconceit be far away !
Through faith we on His Body feed,
Faith only doth the Spirit convey,
And fills our souls with Living Bread ;
The effects of JESU's death imparts,
And pours His Blood into our hearts.

HYMN LXXII.

1 COME, Holy Ghost, thine influence shed,
  And realize the sign ;
Thy Life infuse into the Bread,
  Thy power into the Wine.

2 Effectual let the tokens prove,
  And made by heavenly art
Fit channels to convey Thy love
  To every faithful heart.

HYMN LXXIII.

1 IS not the Cup of Blessing, blest
      By us, the sacred means to impart
   Our Saviour's Blood, with power imprest,
   And pardon to the faithful heart?

2 Is not the hallow'd broken Bread
   A sure communicating sign,
   An Instrument ordain'd to feed
   Our souls with mystic Flesh divine?

3 The effects of His atoning Blood,
   His Body offer'd on the tree,
   Are with the awful types bestow'd
   On me, the pardon'd rebel, *me;*

4 On all who at His word draw near,
   In faith the outward veil look through.
   Sinners, believe; and find Him here:
   Believe; and feel He died for you.

5 In memory of your dying GOD,
   The Symbols faithfully receive,
   And eat the Flesh and drink the Blood
   Of JESUS, and for ever live.

HYMN LXXIV.

1   THIS, this is He that came
      By Water and by Blood!
JESUS is our atoning Lamb,
    Our sanctifying GOD.

2   See from His wounded side
      The mingled current flow!
The Water and the Blood applied
    Shall wash us white as snow.

3   The Water cannot cleanse
      Before the Blood we feel,
To purge the guilt of all our sins,
    And our forgiveness seal.

4   But both in JESUS join,
      Who speaks our sins forgiven,
And gives the purity divine
    That makes us meet for heaven.

HYMN LXXV.

1   FATHER, the grace we claim,
      The double grace bestow'd
On all who trust in Him that came
    By Water and by Blood.

2   Jesu, the Blood apply,
       The righteousness bring in ;
    Us by Thy dying justify,
       And wash out all our sin.

3   Spirit of Faith, come down,
       Thy seal with power set to,
    The Banquet by Thy Presence crown,
       And prove the record true :

4   Pardon and grace impart :
       Come quickly from above,
    And witness now in every heart
       That God is perfect love.

HYMN LXXVI.

1 SEARCHER of hearts, in ours appear,
   And make, and keep them all sincere,
Or draw us burden'd to Thy Son,
Or make Him to His mourners known.

2 Thy promis'd grace vouchsafe to give,
   As each is able to receive ;
The blessed gift to all impart,
Or joy or purity of heart.

3 Our helpless unbelief remove,
And melt us by Thy pardoning love ;
Work in us faith, or faith's increase,
The dawning or the perfect peace.

4 Give each to Thee as seemeth best,
But meet us all at Thy own Feast;
Thy blessing in Thy means convey,
Nor empty send one soul away.

HYMN LXXVII.

1　　HOW long, O LORD, shall we
　　　　In vain lament for Thee ?
Come, and comfort them that mourn,
Come, as in the ancient days,
In Thine Ordinance return,
In Thine own appointed ways.

2　　Come to Thy house again,
　　　Nor let us seek in vain :
This the place of meeting be,
To Thy weeping flock repair,
Let us here Thy beauty see,
Find Thee in the House of Prayer.

3   Let us with solemn awe
        Nigh to Thine Altar draw;
Taste Thee in the broken Bread,
Drink Thee in the mystic Wine;
Now the gracious Spirit shed,
Fill us now with Love Divine.

4   Into our minds recall
        Thy death endur'd for all:
Come in this accepted day,
Come, and all our souls restore,
Come and take our sins away,
Come, and never leave us more.

HYMN LXXVIII.

1   LAMB of God, for whom we languish,
       Make Thy grief our relief;
    Ease us by Thine anguish.

2 O our agonizing Saviour,
      By Thy pain let us gain
      God's eternal favour.

3 Suffer sin no more to oppress us;
      Set us free (all with me);
      By Thy bonds release us.

4 Clear us by Thy condemnation;
   Slain for all, let Thy fall
   Be our exaltation.

5 Thy deserts to us make over;
   Speak us whole, every soul
   By Thy wounds recover.

6 Let us thro' Thy curse inherit
   Blessing's store, love and power,
   Fulness of Thy Spirit.

7 The whole benefit of Thy Passion,
   Present peace, future bliss,
   All Thy great salvation.

8 Power to walk in all well-pleasing,
   Bid us take, come and make
   This the accepted season.

9 In Thine own appointments bless us;
   Meet us here, now appear,
   Our Almighty Jesus.

10 Let the Ordinance be sealing;
   Enter now, claim us Thou
   For Thy constant dwelling.

11 Fill the heart of each believer;
   We are Thine, Love Divine;
   Reign in us for ever.

HYMN LXXIX.

1 JESU, regard the plaintive cry,
　　The groaning of Thy prisoners hear;
Thy Blood to every soul apply,
The heart of every mourner cheer;
The tokens of Thy Passion shew,
And meet us in Thy ways below.

2 The Atonement Thou for all hast made,
O that we all might now receive!
Assure us now the debt is paid,
And Thou hast died that all may live;
Thy Death for all, for us, reveal,
And let Thy Blood *my* pardon seal.

HYMN LXXX.

1 WITH pity, Lord, a sinner see,
　　Weary of Thy ways and Thee;
Forgive my fond despair
A blessing in the means to find,
My struggling to throw off the care,
　　And cast them all behind.

2 Long have I groan'd Thy grace to gain,
　　Suffer'd on, but all in vain;
　　An age of mournful years

I waited for Thy passing by,
And lost my prayers, my sighs, and tears,
    And never found Thee nigh.

3 Thou wouldst not let me go away;
Still Thou forcest me to stay.
        O might the secret power
Which will not with its captive part,·
Nail to the post of mercy's door
        My poor unstable heart!

4 The nails that fix'd Thee to the tree,
Only they can fasten me :
        The death Thou didst endure
For me let it effectual prove :
Thy love alone my soul can cure,
        Thy dear expiring love.

5 Now in the means the grace impart,
Whisper peace into my heart !
        Appear the Justifier
Of all who to Thy Wounds would fly,
And let me have my one desire,
        And see Thy face and die.

HYMN LXXXI.

1   J ESU, we thus obey
       Thy last and kindest word;
Here in Thine own appointed way
       We come to meet our LORD.
       The way Thou hast enjoin'd
       Thou wilt therein appear;
We come with confidence to find
       Thy Special Presence here.

2   Our hearts we open wide
       To make the Saviour room;
And, lo! the Lamb, the Crucified,
       The Sinner's Friend is come!
       His Presence makes the Feast,
       And now our bosoms feel
The glory not to be express'd,
       The joy unspeakable.

3   With pure celestial bliss
       He doth our spirits cheer;
His House of Banqueting is this,
       And He hath brought us here.
       He doth His servants feed
       With Manna from above:
His banner over us is spread,
       His everlasting love.

4   He bids us drink and eat
        Imperishable Food;
He gives His Flesh to be our Meat,
        And bids us drink His Blood:
Whate'er the Almighty can
        To pardon'd sinners give,
The fulness of our GOD made man
        We here with CHRIST receive.

HYMN LXXXII.

1 JESU, Sinner's Friend, receive us,
        Feeble, famishing, and faint;
O Thou Bread of Life, relieve us
        Now, or now we die for want:
Lest we faint, and die for ever,
        Thou our sinking spirits stay;
Give some token of Thy favour;
        Empty send us not away!

2 We have in the desert tarried
        Long, and nothing have to eat;
Comfort us, thro' wandering wearied,
        Feed our souls with living Meat;
Still, with bowels of compassion,
        See Thy helpless people, see;
Let us taste Thy great salvation,
        Let us feed by faith on Thee.

HYMN LXXXIII.

1 LORD, if now Thou passest by us,
  Stand and call us unto Thee;
Freely, fully justify us;
  Give us eyes Thy love to see.
Love, that brought Thee down from heaven,
  Made our GOD a Man of Grief;
Let it shew our sins forgiven;
  Help, O help our unbelief!

2 Long we for Thy love have waited,
  Begging sat by the wayside,
Still we are not new-created,
  Are not wholly sanctified:
Thou to some, in great compassion,
  Hast in part their sight restor'd;
Shew us all Thy full salvation,
  Make the servants as their LORD.

HYMN LXXXIV.

1 CHRIST, our Passover, for us
  Is offer'd up and slain.
Let Him be remember'd thus
  By every soul of man.

We are bound above the rest
His Oblation to proclaim ;
Keep we then the solemn Feast,
   And banquet on the Lamb.

2 Purge we all our sin away,
   That old accursed leaven ;
Sin in us no longer stay,
   In us through CHRIST forgiven :
Let us all, with hearts sincere,
Eat the new unleaven'd Bread,
To our LORD with faith draw near,
   And on His promise feed.

3 JESUS, Master of the Feast,
   The Feast itself Thou art ;
Now receive Thy meanest guest,
   And comfort every heart.
Give us Living Bread to eat,
Manna that from heaven comes down ;
Fill us with Immortal Meat,
   And make Thy nature known.

4 In this barren wilderness
   Thou hast a Table spread,
Furnish'd out with richest grace,
   Whate'er our souls can need.
Still sustain us by Thy love,
Still Thy servants' strength repair,
Till we reach the courts above,
   And feast for ever there.

HYMN LXXXV.

1 O THOU whom sinners love, whose care
    Doth all our sickness heal,
Thee we approach, with hearts sincere;
    Thy power we joy to feel.
To Thee our humblest thanks we pay,
    To Thee our souls we bow,
Of hell erewhile the helpless prey,
    Heirs of Thy glory now.

2 As incense to Thy throne above,
    O let our prayers arise!
Wing with the flames of holy love
    Our living Sacrifice;
Stir up Thy strength, O LORD of might!
    Our willing breasts inspire,
Fill our whole souls with heavenly light,
    Melt with seraphic fire.

3 From Thy bless'd wounds life let us draw;
    Thine all-atoning Blood
Now let us drink, with trembling awe;
    Thy Flesh be now our Food.
Come, LORD, Thy sovereign aid impart;
    Here make Thy likeness shine;
Stamp Thy whole image on our heart,
    And all our heart is Thine.

HYMN LXXXVI.

1　　AND shall I let Him go?
　　　　If now I do not *feel*
　The streams of Living Water flow,
　　Shall I forsake the Well?

2　　Because He hides His face,
　　　Shall I no longer stay,
　But leave the channels of His grace,
　　And cast the means away?

3　　Get thee behind me, Fiend,
　　　On others try thy skill,
　Here let thy hellish whispers end,
　　To thee I say, *Be still !*

4　　Jesus hath spoke the Word,
　　　His will my reason is,
　Do this in memory of thy Lord,
　　Jesus hath said, *Do this !*

5　　He bids me eat the Bread,
　　　He bids me drink the Wine ;
　No other motive, Lord, I need,
　　No other Word than Thine.

6   I cheerfully comply
       With what my LORD doth say;
Let others ask a reason why,
       My glory is to obey.

7   His will is good and just:
       Shall I His will withstand?
If JESUS bids me lick the dust,
       I bow at His command:

8   Because He saith, *Do this,*
       This I will always do,
Till JESUS come in glorious bliss
       I *thus* His death will *shew.*

HYMN LXXXVII.

1 BY the Picture of thy Passion
       Still in pain I remain
Waiting for salvation.

2 JESU, let Thy sufferings ease me,
       Saviour, LORD, speak the word,
By Thy death release me.

3 At Thy Cross behold me lying,
       Make my soul throughly whole
By Thy Blood's applying.

4 Hear me, LORD, my sins confessing,
　　Now relieve, Saviour give,
　Give me now Thy blessing.

5 Still my cruel sins oppress me,
　　Tied and bound till the sound
　Of Thy voice release me.

6 Call me out of condemnation,
　　To my grave come and save,
　Save me by Thy Passion.

7 To Thy foul and helpless creature
　　Come, and cleanse all my sins,
　Come and change my nature.

8 Save me now, and still deliver ;
　　Enter in, cast out sin :
　Keep Thine house for ever.

HYMN LXXXVIII.

1 GIVE us this day, all-bounteous LORD,
　　　Our Sacramental Bread,
　Who thus His Sacrifice record
　　That suffer'd in our stead.

2 Reveal in every soul Thy Son,
　　And let us taste the grace
Which brings assur'd salvation down
　　To all who seek Thy face.

3 Who here commemorate His death
　　To us His life impart;
The loving filial spirit breathe
　　Into my waiting heart.

4 My earnest of eternal bliss
　　Let my Redeemer be,
And if e'en now He present is,
　　Now let Him speak in me.

HYMN LXXXIX.

1 YE faithful souls who thus record
　　　The Passion of that Lamb Divine,
Is the Memorial of your LORD
An useless form, an empty sign?
Or doth He here His life impart?
What saith the Witness in your heart?

2 Is it the dying Master's will
That we should this persist to do?
Then let Him here Himself reveal,
The tokens of His Presence shew,
Descend in blessings from above,
And answer by the fire of love.

3 Who Thee remember in Thy ways,
  Come, LORD, and meet and bless us here ;
  In confidence we ask the grace,
  Faithful and True, appear, appear :
  Let all perceive Thy blood applied,
  Let all discern the Crucified.

4 'Tis done ; the LORD sets to His seal ;
  The prayer is heard, the grace is given ;
  With joy unspeakable we feel
  The Holy Ghost sent down from Heaven :
  The Altar streams with sacred Blood,
  And all the Temple flames with GOD !

HYMN XC.

1 BLEST be the love, for ever blest,
    The bleeding love we thus record !
  JESUS, we take the dear bequest,
  Obedient to Thy kindest word ;
  Thy word which stands divinely sure,
  And shall from age to age endure.

2 In vain the subtle Tempter tries
  Thy dying precept to repeal,
  To hide the letter from our eyes,
  And break the testamental seal,
  Refine the solid truth away,
  And make us free—to disobey.

3 In vain he labours to persuade
Thou didst not mean the word should bind:
The Feast for Thy first followers made,
For them and us and all mankind,
Mindful of Thee we still attend,
And this we do, till Time shall end.

4 Thro' vain pretence of clearer light
We do not, LORD, refuse to see,
Or weakly the commandment slight
To shew our Christian liberty,
Or seek rebelliously to prove
The pureness of our catholic love.

5 Our wandering brethren's hearts to gain
We will not let our Saviour go,
But in Thine ancient paths remain,
But thus persist Thy death to shew,
Till strong with all Thy life we rise,
And meet Thee coming in the skies!

HYMN XCI.

1 ALL-LOVING, all-redeeming LORD,
   Thy wandering sheep with pity see,
Who slight Thy dearest dying word,
And will not thus remember Thee;
To all who would perform Thy will
The glorious promis'd truth reveal.

2 Can we enjoy Thy richest love,
  Nor long that they the grace may share?
  Thou from their eyes the scales remove,
  Thou the Eternal Word declare,
  Thy Spirit with Thy Word impart,
  And speak the precept to their heart.

3 If chiefly here Thou may'st be found,
  If now, e'en now, we find Thee here,
  O let their joys like ours abound ;
  Invite them to the Royal Cheer,
  Feed with imperishable Food,
  And fill their raptur'd souls with GOD.

4 JESU, we will not let Thee go,
  But keep herein our fastest hold,
  Till Thou to them Thy counsel shew,
  And call and make us all one fold,
  One hallow'd undivided Bread,
  One body knit to Thee our Head.

HYMN XCII.

1   AH, tell us no more
         The spirit and power
      Of JESUS our GOD
  Is not to be found in this life-giving Food !

2   Did Jesus ordain
His Supper in vain,
And furnish a Feast
For none but His earliest servants to taste?

3   Nay, but this is His will
(We know it and feel)
That *we* should partake
The Banquet for all He so freely did make.

4   In rapturous bliss
He bids us do this ;
The joy it imparts
Hath witness'd His gracious design in our hearts.

5   'Tis God we believe,
Who cannot deceive ;
The witness of God
Is present, and speaks in the mystical Blood.

6   Receiving the Bread,
On Jesus we feed :
It doth not appear
His manner of working ; but Jesus is here !

7   With Bread from above,
With comfort and love,
Our spirit He fills,
And all His unspeakable goodness reveals.

8   O that all men would haste
          To the spiritual Feast,
          At Jesus's word
Do this, and be fed with the love of our Lord !

9   True Light of mankind,
          Shine into their mind,
          And clearly reveal
Thy perfect, and good, and acceptable will.

10   Bring near the glad day
          When all shall obey
          Thy dying request,
And eat of Thy Supper and lean on Thy breast.

11   To all men impart
          One way and one heart ;
          Thy people be shewn
All righteous and sinless and perfect in One.

12   Then, then let us see
          Thy glory, and be
          Caught up in the air
This heavenly Supper in heaven to share.

III. *The* SACRAMENT *a Pledge of* HEAVEN.

HYMN XCIII.

1

COME, let us join with one accord,
Who share the Supper of the LORD,
    Our LORD and Master's praise to sing.
Nourish'd on earth with Living Bread,
We now are at His Table fed,
    But wait to see our heavenly King:
To see the great Invisible
Without a Sacramental veil,
    With all His robes of glory on;
In rapturous joy and love and praise,
Him to behold with open face,
    High on His everlasting throne!

2 The Wine which doth His Passion shew,
We soon with Him shall drink it new
    In yonder dazzling courts above;
Admitted to the heavenly Feast,
We shall His choicest blessings taste,
    And banquet on His richest love.
We soon the midnight cry shall hear,
Arise, and meet the Bridegroom near;

The marriage of the Lamb is come :
Attended by His heavenly friends,
The glorious King of saints descends
   To take His bride in triumph home.

3 Then let us still in hope rejoice,
And listen for the archangel's voice
   Loud echoing to the trump of God ;
Haste to the dreadful, joyful day,
When heaven and earth shall flee away,
   By all-devouring flames destroyed :
While we from out the burnings fly,
With eagles' wings mount up on high,
   Where Jesus is on *Sion* seen ;
'Tis there He for our coming waits,
And, lo, the everlasting gates
   Lift up their heads to take us in !

4 By faith and hope already there,
Ev'n now the marriage Feast we share,
   Ev'n now we by the Lamb are fed ;
Our Lord's celestial joy we prove,
Led by the spirit of His love,
   To springs of living comfort led :
Suffering, and curse, and death are o'er,
And pain afflicts the soul no more
   While harbour'd in the Saviour's breast ;
He quiets all our plaints and cries,
And wipes the sorrow from our eyes,
   And lulls us in His arms to rest !

HYMN XCIV.

1 O WHAT a soul-transporting Feast
   Doth this Communion yield !
Remembering here Thy Passion past,
   We with Thy love are fill'd.

2 Sure instrument of present grace
   Thy Sacrament we find ;
Yet higher blessings it displays,
   And raptures still behind.

3 It bears us now on eagle's wings,
   If Thou the power impart,
And Thee our glorious earnest brings
   Into our faithful heart.

4 O let us still the earnest feel,
   The unutterable peace ;
This loving spirit be the seal
   Of our eternal bliss !

HYMN XCV.

1 IN Jesus we live, in Jesus we rest,
   And thankful receive His dying Bequest ;
The Cup of Salvation His mercy bestows,
And all from His Passion our happiness flows.

2 With mystical Wine He comforts us here,
And gladly we join till JESUS appear,
With hearty thanksgiving His death to record;
The living, the living, should sing of their LORD.

3 He hallow'd the Cup which now we receive,
The pledge of our hope with JESUS to live,
(Where sorrow and sadness shall never be found)
With glory and gladness eternally crown'd.

4 The fruit of the vine (the joy it implies)
Again we shall join to drink in the skies,
Exult in His favour, our triumph renew;
And I, saith the Saviour, will drink it with you.

HYMN XCVI.

1 HAPPY the souls to JESUS join'd,
    And sav'd by grace alone,
Walking in all Thy ways we find
    Our heaven on earth begun.

2 The Church triumphant in Thy love,
    Their mighty joys we know;
They sing the Lamb in hymns above,
    And we in hymns below.

3 Thee in Thy glorious realm they praise,
   And bow before Thy throne,
We in the kingdom of Thy grace,—
   The kingdoms are but one.

4 The Holy to the Holiest leads,
   From hence our spirits rise,
And he that in Thy statutes treads
   Shall meet Thee in the skies.

HYMN XCVII.

1 THEE, King of Saints, we praise,
   For this our Living Bread;
Nourish'd by Thy preserving grace,
   And at Thy Table fed;

2   Who in these lower parts
   Of Thy great kingdom feast,
We feel the earnest in our hearts
   Of our eternal rest.

3   Yet still a higher seat
   We in Thy kingdom claim,
Who here begin by faith to eat
   The Supper of the Lamb.

4 That glorious heavenly prize
  We surely shall attain,
And in the palace of the skies
  With Thee for ever reign.

HYMN XCVIII.

1 WHERE shall this Memorial end?
  Thither let our souls ascend,
Live on earth to heaven restor'd,
Wait the coming of our LORD.

2 JESUS terminates our hope,
Jesus is our wishes' scope;
End of this great Mystery,
Him we fain would die to see.

3 He whom we remember here,
CHRIST, shall in the clouds appear;
Manifest to every eye,
We shall soon behold Him nigh.

4 Faith ascends the mountain's height,
Now enjoys the pompous sight,
Antedates the final doom,
Sees the Judge in glory come.

5 Lo, He comes triumphant down,
  Seated on His great white throne;
  Cherubs bear it on their wings,
  Shouting, bear the King of kings.

6 Lo, His glorious banner spread,
  Stains the skies with deepest red,
  Dyes the land, and fires the wood,
  Turns the ocean into blood.

7 Gather'd to the well-known Sign,
  We our elder brethren join,
  Swiftly to our LORD fly up,
  Hail Him on the mountain-top;

8 Take our happy seats above,
  Banquet on His heavenly love,
  Lean on our Redeemer's breast,
  In His arms for ever rest.

HYMN XCIX.

1 WHITHER should our full souls aspire
    At this transporting Feast?
They never can on earth be higher,
  Or more completely blest.

2 Our Cup of Blessing from above
    Delightfully runs o'er;
Till from these bodies they remove,
    Our souls can hold no more.

3 To heaven the mystic Banquet leads,
    Let us to heaven ascend,
And bear this joy upon our heads
    Till it in glory end;

4 Till all who truly join in this,
    The Marriage Supper share,
Enter into their Master's bliss,
    And feast for ever there.

HYMN C.

1 RETURNING to His throne above,
    The Friend of sinners cried,
Do this in memory of My love:
    He spoke the word, and died.

2 He tasted death for every one;
    The Saviour of mankind
Out of our sight to heaven is gone,
    But left His Pledge behind.

3 His Sacramental Pledge we take,
    Nor will we let it go;
Till in the clouds our LORD comes back,
    We thus His death will shew.

4 Come quickly, LORD, for whom we mourn,
    And comfort all that grieve;
Prepare the Bride, and then return,
    And to Thyself receive.

5 Now to Thy glorious kingdom come
    (Thou hast a Token given),
And while Thine arms receive us home,
    Recall Thy Pledge in heaven.

HYMN CI.

1 HOW glorious is the life above
    Which in this Ordinance we *taste;*
That fulness of celestial love,
That joy which shall for ever last!

2 That heavenly life in CHRIST conceal'd
These earthen vessels could not bear,
The part which now we find reveal'd
No tongue of angels can declare.

3 The Light of Life eternal darts
   Into our souls a dazzling ray;
   A drop of heaven o'erflows our hearts,
   And deluges the house of clay.

4 Sure pledge of ecstacies unknown
   Shall this divine Communion be;
   The ray shall rise into a sun,
   The drop shall swell into a sea.

HYMN CII.

1 O THE length, and breadth, and height,
       And depth of dying love!
   Love that turns our faith to sight,
       And wafts to heaven above.
   Pledge of our possession this,
   This which Nature faints to bear;
   Who shall then support the bliss,
       The joy, the rapture there!

2 Flesh and blood shall not receive
       The vast inheritance;
   God we cannot see, and live
       The life of feeble sense.
   In our weakest nonage, here,
   Up into our Head we grow,
   Saints before our Lord appear,
       And ripe for heaven below.

3 We His image shall regain,
  And to His stature rise,
Rise unto a perfect man,
  And then ascend the skies;
Find our happy mansions there,
Strong to bear the joys above,
All the glorious weight to bear
  Of everlasting love.

HYMN CIII.

1 TAKE and eat, the Saviour saith,
  This My sacred Body is!
Him we take and eat by faith,
Feed upon that Flesh of His;
All the benefits receive
Which His Passion did procure;
Pardon'd by His grace we live,
Grace which makes salvation sure.

2 Title to eternal bliss,
Here His precious death we find;
This the pledge, the earnest this
Of the purchas'd joys behind:
Here He gives our souls a taste,
Heaven into our hearts He pours:
Still believe, and hold Him fast;
GOD, and CHRIST, and all is ours!

HYMN CIV.

1 RETURNING to His Father's throne,
      Hear all the interceding Son,
   And join in that eternal prayer :
   He prays that we with Him may reign,
   And He that did the kingdom gain
      For us, shall soon conduct us there.

2 "I will that those Thou giv'st to Me
      May all My heavenly glory see,
         But first be perfected in One."
   Amen, Amen, our heart replies ;
   Prepare, and take us to the skies ;
      Thy prayer be heard, Thy will be done.

HYMN CV.

1 LIFT your eyes of faith, and see
      Saints and angels join'd in one,
   What a countless company
   Stands before yon dazzling throne !
   Each before his Saviour stands,
   All in milk-white robes array'd,
   Palms they carry in their hands,
   Crowns of glory on their head.

2 Saints, begin the endless song,
  Cry aloud in heavenly lays ;
  Glory doth to God belong,
  God the glorious Saviour praise.
  All from Him salvation came,
  Him who reigns enthron'd on high ;
  Glory to the bleeding Lamb,
  Let the morning stars reply.

3 Angel-powers the throne surround,
  Next the saints in glory they ;
  Lull'd with the transporting sound,
  They their silent homage pay :
  Prostrate on their face before
  God and His Messiah fall,
  Then in hymns of praise adore,
  Shout the Lamb that died for all.

4 Be it so, they all reply,
  Him let all our orders praise ;
  Him that did for sinners die,
  Saviour of the favour'd race :
  Render we our God His right,
  Glory, wisdom, thanks, and power,
  Honour, majesty, and might ;
  Praise Him, praise Him evermore !

HYMN CVI.

1 WHAT are these array'd in white,
  Brighter than the noon-day sun,
Foremost of the sons of light,
Nearest the eternal throne?
These are they that bore the cross,
Nobly for their Master stood,
Sufferers in His righteous cause,
Followers of the dying GOD.

2 Out of great distress they came,
Wash'd their robes by faith below
In the Blood of yonder Lamb,
Blood that washes white as snow.
Therefore are they next the throne,
Serve their Maker day and night;
GOD resides among His own,
GOD doth in His saints delight.

3 More than conquerors at last,
Here they find their trials o'er;
They have all their sufferings past,
Hunger now and thirst no more;
No excessive heat they feel
From the sun's directer ray;
In a milder clime they dwell,
Region of eternal day.

4 He that on the throne doth reign,
  Them the Lamb shall always feed,
  With the Tree of Life sustain,
  To the living fountains lead ;
  He shall all their sorrows chase,
  All their wants at once remove,
  Wipe the tears from every face,
  Fill up every soul with love.

HYMN CVII.

1 ALL hail ! Thou suffering Son of God,
  Who didst these mysteries ordain,
  Communion of Thy Flesh and Blood,
  Sure instrument Thy grace to gain,
  Type of the heavenly Marriage-Feast,
  Pledge of our everlasting rest.

2 Jesu, Thine own with pity see,
  Our helpless unbelief remove,
  Empower us to remember Thee,
  Give us the faith that works by love ;
  The faith which Thou hast given increase,
  And seal us up in glorious peace.

IIYMN CVIII.

1 AH! give us, Saviour, to partake
   The sufferings which this Emblem shews ;
Thy Flesh our food immortal make ;
Thy Blood, which in this channel flows,
In all its benefits impart,
And sanctify our sprinkled heart.

2 For all that joy which now we taste,
Our happy hallow'd souls prepare ;
O let us hold the earnest fast,
This Pledge that we Thy heaven shall share,
Shall drink it new with Thee above,
The Wine of Thy eternal love.

HYMN CIX.

1 LORD, Thou know'st my simpleness,
   All my groans are heard by Thee ;
See me hungering after grace,
Gasping at Thy table see
One who would in Thee believe,
Would with joy the crumbs receive.

2 Look as when Thy closing eye
  Saw the thief beside Thy Cross;
Thou art now gone up on high,
  Undertake my desperate cause;
In Thy heavenly kingdom Thou,
Be the Friend of sinners now.

3 Saviour, Prince, enthron'd above,
  Send a peaceful answer down;
Let the bowels of Thy love
  Echo to a sinner's groan,
One who feebly thinks of Thee,
Thou for good remember me.

HYMN CX.

1   JESU, on Thee we feed
     Along the desert way;
Thou art the Living Bread,
  Which doth our spirits stay;
And all who in this Banquet join
Lean on the Staff of Life Divine.

2   While to Thy upper courts
     We take our joyful flight,
Thy blessed Cross supports
  Each feeble *Israelite;*
Like hoary dying *Jacob,* we
Lean on our staff and worship Thee.

3   O may we still abide
In Thee our pardoning GOD,
Thy Spirit be our guide,
Thy Body be our food,
Till Thou who hast the Token given
Shalt bear us on Thyself to heaven.

HYMN CXI.

1   AND can we call to mind
The Lamb for sinners slain,
And not expect to find
What He for us did gain,
What GOD to us in Him hath given,
Pardon, and holiness, and heaven?

2   We now forgiveness have,
We feel His work begun,
And He shall fully save
And perfect us in one;
Shall soon, in all His image drest,
Receive us to the Marriage-Feast.

3   This Token of Thy love
We thankfully receive,
And hence with joy remove
With Thee in heaven to live;
There, LORD, we shall Thy pledge restore,
And live to praise Thee evermore.

HYMN CXII.

1 ETERNAL Spirit, gone up on high,
   Blessings for mortals to receive,
Send down those blessings from the sky,
To us Thy gifts and graces give.
With holy things our mouths are fill'd,
O let our hearts with joy o'erflow ;
Descend in pardoning love reveal'd,
And meet us in Thy courts below.

2 Thy Sacrifice without the gate
Once offer'd up we call to mind,
And humbly at Thy Altar wait
Our interest in Thy death to find :
We thirst to drink Thy precious Blood,
We languish in Thy wounds to rest,
And hunger for immortal food,
And long on all Thy love to feast.

3 O that we now Thy Flesh may eat,
Its virtues really receive,
Empower'd by this Immortal Meat
The life of holiness to live :
Partakers of Thy Sacrifice,
O may we all Thy nature share,
Till to the holiest place we rise,
And keep the Feast for ever there !

HYMN CXIII.

1 GIVE us, O Lord, the children's Bread,
     By ministerial angels fed
  (The angels of Thy Church below);
Nourish us with preserving grace
Our forty years or forty days,
  And lead us through the vale of woe.

2 Strengthen'd by this Immortal Food,
O let us reach the Mount of God,
  And face to face our Saviour see;
In songs of praise and love and joy,
With all Thy first-born sons employ
  A happy whole eternity.

HYMN CXIV.

1 SEE there the quickening cause of all
     Who live the life of grace beneath!
God caus'd on Him the sleep to fall,
And, lo, His eyes are closed in death!

2 He sleeps; and from His open side
The mingled Blood and Water flow;
They both give being to His Bride,
And wash His Church as white as snow.

3 True principles of Life Divine,
  Issues from these the second *Eve*,
  Mother of all the faithful line,
  Of all that by His passion live.

4 O what a miracle of love
  Hath He, our heavenly *Adam*, shew'd!
  JESUS forsook His throne above,
  That we might all be born of GOD.

5 'Twas not an useless rib He lost,
  His heart's last drop of Blood He gave;
  His life, His precious life, it cost
  Our dearly ransom'd souls to save.

6 And will He not His purchase take,
  Who died to make us all His own,
  One spirit with Himself to make,
  Flesh of His flesh, bone of His bone?

7 He will, our hearts reply, He will:
  He hath e'en here a token given,
  And bids us meet Him on the hill,
  And keep the Marriage-Feast in heaven.

HYMN CXV.

1 O GLORIOUS instrument Divine
    Which blessings to our souls conveys,
  Brings with the hallow'd Bread and Wine
  His strengthening and refreshing grace,
  Presents His Bleeding Sacrifice,
  His all-reviving death applies!

2 Glory to GOD who reigns above,
  But suffer'd once for man below;
  With joy we celebrate His love,
  And thus His precious Passion shew,
  Till in the clouds our LORD we see,
  And shout with all His saints, 'TIS HE!

IV. *The* HOLY EUCHARIST *as it implies a Sacrifice.*

HYMN CXVI.

1

VICTIM Divine, Thy grace we claim
While thus Thy precious death we shew ;
Once offer'd up a spotless Lamb
In Thy great temple here below,
Thou didst for all mankind atone,
And standest now before the throne.

2 Thou standest in the holiest place,
As now for guilty sinners slain ;
Thy Blood of Sprinkling speaks and prays
All-prevalent for helpless man ;
Thy Blood is still our ransom found,
And spreads salvation all around.

3 The smoke of Thy atonement here
Darken'd the sun and rent the vail,
Made the new way to heaven appear,
And shew'd the Great Invisible ;
Well-pleas'd in Thee our GOD looked down,
And call'd His rebels to a crown.

4 He still respects Thy Sacrifice,
   Its savour sweet doth always please ;
   The Offering smokes through earth and skies,
   Diffusing life and joy and peace ;
   To these Thy lower courts it comes,
   And fills them with divine perfumes.

5 We need not now go up to heaven
   To bring the long-sought Saviour down ;
   Thou art to all already given,
   Thou dost e'en now Thy Banquet crown :
   To every faithful soul appear,
   And shew Thy Real Presence here.

HYMN CXVII.

1 THOU Lamb that suffer'dst on the tree,
      And in this dreadful Mystery
   Still offer'st up Thyself to God,
We cast us on Thy Sacrifice,
Wrapt in the sacred smoke arise,
   And cover'd with the atoning Blood.

2 Thy Death presented in our stead
   Enters us now among the dead,
      Parts of Thy mystic Body here ;
   By Thy Divine Oblation rais'd,
   And on our *Aaron's* ephod plac'd,
      We now with Thee in heaven appear.

3 Thy Death exalts Thy ransom'd ones,
And sets amidst the precious stones,
  Closest Thy dear, Thy loving breast,
Israel as on Thy shoulders stands ;
Our names are graven on the hands,
  The heart, of our Eternal Priest.

4 For us He ever intercedes,
His heaven-deserving Passion pleads,
  Presenting us before the throne ;
We want no sacrifice beside,
By that great Offering sanctified,
  One with our Head, for ever one.

HYMN CXVIII.

1   LIVE our eternal Priest
        By men and angels blest !
JESUS CHRIST, the Crucified,
He who did for us atone,
From the Cross where once He died,
Now He up to heaven is gone.

2   He ever lives, and prays
        For all the faithful race ;
In the holiest place above
Sinners' advocate He stands,
Pleads for us His dying love,
Shews for us His bleeding hands.

3   His Body torn and rent
      He doth to God present:
In that dear Memorial shews
Israel's chosen tribes imprest:
All our names the Father knows,
Reads them on our *Aaron's* breast.

4   He reads while we beneath
      Present our Saviour's death,
Do as JESUS bids us do,
Signify His Flesh and Blood,
Him in a Memorial shew,
Offer up the Lamb to GOD.

5   From this thrice-hallow'd shade,
      Which JESU's Cross hath made,
Image of His Sacrifice,
Never, never will we move,
Till with all His saints we rise,
Rise, and take our place above.

HYMN CXIX.

1 FATHER, GOD, who seest in me
      Only sin and misery,
See Thine own Anointed One,
Look on Thy beloved Son.

2 Turn from me Thy glorious eyes
To that Bloody Sacrifice,
To the full atonement made,
To the utmost ransom paid ;

3 To the Blood that speaks above,
Calls for Thy forgiving love ;
To the tokens of His death,
Here exhibited beneath.

4 Hear His Blood's prevailing cry,
Let Thy bowels then reply,
Then thro' Him the sinner see,
Then in JESUS look on me.

HYMN CXX.

1 FATHER, see the Victim slain,
JESUS CHRIST the just, the good,
Offer'd up for guilty man,
Pouring out His precious Blood ;
Him and then the sinner see,
Look thro' JESU's wounds on me.

2 Me, the sinner most distrest,
Most afflicted and forlorn ;
Stranger to a moment's rest,
Rueing that I e'er was born ;
Pierc'd with sin's invenom'd dart,
Dying of a broken heart.

3 Dying, whom Thy hands have made
All Thy Blessings to receive;
Dying, whom Thy love hath stay'd,
Whom Thy pity would have live;
Dying at my Saviour's side,
Dying for whom CHRIST hath died.

4 Can it, Father, can it be?
What doth JESU's Blood reply?
If it doth not plead for me,
Let my soul for ever die;
But if mine thro' Him Thou art,
Speak the pardon to my heart.

HYMN CXXI.

1 FATHER, behold Thy favourite Son,
The glorious partner of Thy throne,
For ever plac'd at Thy right hand;
O look on Thy MESSIAH's face,
And seal the covenant of Thy grace
To us who in Thy JESUS stand.

2 To us Thou hast redemption sent;
And we again to Thee present
The Blood that speaks our sins forgiven,
That sprinkles all the nation round;
And now Thou hear'st the solemn sound
Loud echoing thro' the courts of heaven.

3 The Cross on *Calvary* He bore,
He suffer'd once to die no more,
   But left a sacred Pledge behind:
See here !—it on Thy Altar lies,
Memorial of the Sacrifice
   He offer'd once for all mankind.

4 Father, the grand Oblation see,
The death as present now with Thee,
   As when He gasp'd on earth—*Forgive !*
Answer, and shew the curse remov'd,
Accept us in the Well-belov'd,
   And bid Thy world of rebels live.

HYMN CXXII.

1 FATHER, let the sinner go,
   The Lamb did once atone ;
Lo ! we to Thy justice shew
   The Passion of Thy Son :
Thus to Thee we set it forth :
He the dying precept gave,
He that hath sufficient worth
   A thousand worlds to save.

2 Can Thy justice aught reply
   To our prevailing plea ?
Jesus died Thy grace to buy
   For all mankind, and me ;

Still before Thy righteous throne
Stands the Lamb as newly slain :
Canst Thou turn away Thy Son,
   Or let Him bleed in vain ?

3 Still the Wounds are open wide,
   The Blood doth freely flow,
As when first His sacred side
   Receiv'd the deadly blow :
Still, O God, the Blood is warm,
Cover'd with the Blood we are ;
Find a part it doth not arm,
   And strike the sinner there !

HYMN CXXIII.

1 O THOU, whose offering on the tree
   The legal offerings all foreshew'd,
Borrow'd their whole effects from Thee,
And drew their virtue from Thy Blood :
The blood of goats and bullocks slain
Could never for our sin atone ;
To purge the guilty offerer's stain
Thine was the work, and *Thine* alone.

2 Vain in themselves their duties were ;
   Their services could never please,
Till join'd with Thine, and made to share
The merits of Thy righteousness :

Forward they cast a faithful look
On Thy approaching Sacrifice,
And thence their pleasing savour took,
And rose accepted in the skies.

3 Those feeble types and shadows old
Are all in Thee, the Truth, fulfill'd,
And thro' this Sacrament we hold
The Substance in our hearts reveal'd ;
By faith we see Thy sufferings past
In this mysterious Rite brought back,
And, on Thy grand Oblation cast,
Its saving benefit partake.

4 Memorial of Thy Sacrifice,
This Eucharistic Mystery
The full atoning grace supplies,
And sanctifies our gifts in Thee :
Our persons and performance please,
While God in Thee looks down from heaven
Our acceptable service sees,
And whispers all our sins forgiven.

HYMN CXXIV.

1 ALL hail, Redeemer of mankind !
  Thy life on *Calvary* resign'd
  Did fully once for all atone ;
Thy Blood hath paid our utmost price,
Thine all-sufficient Sacrifice
  Remains eternally alone.

2 Angels and men might strive in vain,
  They could not add the smallest grain
    To augment Thy death's atoning power :
  The Sacrifice is all complete,
  'The death Thou never canst repeat,
    Once offer'd up to die no more.

3 Yet may we celebrate below,
  And daily thus Thine Offering shew,
    Expos'd before Thy Father's eyes ;
  In this tremendous Mystery
  Present Thee bleeding on the Tree,
    Our everlasting Sacrifice.

4 Father, behold Thy dying Son !
  E'en now He lays our ransom down,
    E'en now declares our sins forgiven :
  His Flesh is rent, the living way
  Is open'd to eternal day,
    And, lo, thro' Him we pass to heaven !

HYMN CXXV.

1 O GOD of our forefathers, hear,
   And make Thy faithful mercies known;
To Thee thro' Jesus we draw near,
Thy suffering, well-beloved Son,
In whom Thy smiling face we see,
In whom Thou art well-pleased with me.

2 With solemn faith we offer up,
And spread before Thy glorious eyes
That only ground of all our hope,
That precious, bleeding Sacrifice,
Which brings Thy grace on sinners down,
And perfects all our souls in One.

3 Acceptance thro' His only Name,
Forgiveness in His Blood we have;
But more abundant life we claim
Thro' Him who died our souls to save,
To sanctify us by His Blood,
And fill with all the life of God

4 Father, behold Thy dying Son,
And hear His Blood that speaks above;
On us let all Thy grace be shewn,
Peace, righteousness, and joy, and love:
Thy kingdom come to every heart,
And all Thou hast, and all Thou art.

HYMN CXXVI.

1 FATHER, to Him we turn our face,
      Who did for all atone,
And worship toward Thy holy place,
      And seek Thee in Thy Son.

2 Him, the true Ark and Mercy-seat,
      By faith we call to mind,
Faith in the Blood atoning yet
      For us and all mankind.

3 To Thee His Passion we present,
      Who for our ransom dies;
We reach by this great instrument
      The Eternal Sacrifice.

4 The Lamb as crucified afresh
      Is here held out to men;
The tokens of His Blood and Flesh
      Are on this Table seen.

5 The Lamb His Father now surveys,
      As on this Altar slain,
Its bleeding and imploring grace
      For every soul of man.

6 Father, for us, e'en us, He bleeds,
      The Sacrifice receive:
Forgive, for Jesus intercedes;
      He gasps in death—Forgive!

HYMN CXXVII.

1 DID Thine ancient *Israel* go
   With solemn praise and prayer
To Thy hallow'd courts below
   To meet and serve Thee there?
To Thy Body, LORD, we flee;
This the Consecrated Shrine,
Temple of the Deity,
   The real House Divine.

2 Did they toward the Altar turn
   Their hopes, their heart, and face,
Whence the victim's blood was borne
   Into the holiest place?
Toward the Cross we still look up,
Toward the Lamb for sinners given;
Thro' Thine only death we hope
   To find our way to heaven.

HYMN CXXVIII.

1

ALL hail, Thou mighty to atone!
To expiate sin is Thine alone;
    Thou hast alone the wine-press trod,
    Thou only hast for sinners died,
By one Oblation satisfied
    The inexorably righteous GOD.

2 Should the whole Church in flames arise,
Offer'd as one burnt-sacrifice,
    The sinner's smallest debt to pay,
They could not, LORD, Thine honour share,
With Thee the Father's justice bear,
    Or bear one single sin away.

3 Thyself our utmost price hast paid,
Thou hast for all atonement made,
    For all the sins of all mankind:
GOD doth in Thee redemption give:
But how shall we the grace receive?
    But how shall we the blessing find?

4 We only can *accept* the grace,
  And humbly our Redeemer praise
    Who bought the glorious liberty:
  The life Thou didst for all procure
  We make by our believing sure
    To us who live and die to Thee.

5 While faith the atoning Blood applies,
  Ourselves a living sacrifice
    We freely offer up to God:
  And none but those His glory share
  Who crucified with Jesus are,
    And follow where their Saviour trod.

6 Saviour, to Thee our lives we give;
  Our meanest sacrifice receive,
    And to Thine own Oblation join:
  Our suffering and triumphant Head,
  Thro' all Thy states Thy members lead,
    And seat us on the Throne Divine.

HYMN CXXIX.

1   SEE where our great High Priest
      Before the Lord appears,
  And on His loving breast
  The tribes of *Israel* bears,
Never without His people seen,
The Head of all believing men!

2   With Him, the Corner-Stone,
       The living stones conjoin;
       CHRIST and His Church are one,
       One Body and one Vine:
For us He uses all His powers,
And all He has, or is, is ours.

3   The motions of our Head
       The members all pursue,
       By His good Spirit led
       To act, and suffer too,
Whate'er He did on earth sustain,
Till glorious all like Him we reign.

HYMN CXXX.

1   J ESU, we follow Thee,
         In all Thy footsteps tread,
And pant for full conformity
       To our exalted Head.

2   We would, we would partake
       Thy every state below,
And suffer all things for Thy sake,
       And to Thy glory do.

3   We in Thy birth are born,
        Sustain Thy grief and loss,
Share in Thy want, and shame, and scorn,
        And die upon Thy Cross.

4   Baptiz'd into Thy death,
        We sink into Thy grave,
Till Thou the quickening Spirit breathe,
        And to the utmost save.

5   Thou saidst, " Where'er I am,
        There shall my servant be."
Master, the welcome word we claim,
        And die to live with Thee.

6   To us who share Thy pain,
        Thy joy shall soon be given,
And we shall in Thy glory reign,
        For Thou art now in heaven.

HYMN CXXXI.

1   WOULD the Saviour of mankind
            Without His people die?
No, to Him we all are join'd
        As more than standers-by.

Freely as the Victim came
To the Altar of His Cross,
We attend the slaughtered Lamb,
  And suffer for His cause.

2 Him e'en now by faith we see :
    Before our eyes He stands!
On the suffering Deity
    We lay our trembling hands,
Lay our sins upon His head,
Wait on the dread Sacrifice,
Feel the lovely Victim bleed,
    And die while JESUS dies !

3 Sinners, see, He dies for all,
    And feel His mortal wound ;
Prostrate on your faces fall,
    And kiss the hallow'd ground ;
Hallow'd by the streaming Blood,
Blood whose virtue all may know,
Sharers with the dying GOD,
    And crucified below.

4 Sprinkled with the Blood we lie,
    And bless its cleansing power,
Crying in the Spirit's cry,
    Our Saviour we adore !
JESU, LORD, whose Cross we bear,
Let Thy death our sins destroy,
Make us who Thy sorrow share
    Partakers of Thy joy.

HYMN CXXXII.

1   LET heaven and earth proclaim
      Our common Saviour's name,
Offer'd by Himself to GOD
In His temple here beneath,
Him who shed for all His Blood,
Him for all who tasted death.

2   By faith e'en now we see
      The suffering Deity,
At the head of whole mankind,
Lo! He comes for all to die;
Not a soul is left behind
Whom He did not love and buy.

3   Firstborn of many sons,
      His Blood for us atones,
Saves us from the mortal pain,
If we by His Cross abide,
If we in the House remain
Where our Elder Brother died.

HYMN CXXXIII.

1   O THOU, who hast our sorrows took,
      Who all our sins didst singly bear,

To Thy dear Bloody Cross we look,
We cast us on Thy Offering there ;
For pardon on Thy death rely,
For grace and strength to reach the sky.

2 We look on Thee, our dying Lamb,
On Thee whom we have pierc'd, and mourn ;
Partakers of Thy grief and shame,
Thy anguish hath our bosoms torn :
For us Thou didst Thy life resign ;
Was ever love or grief like Thine !

3 O what a killing thought is this,
A sword to pierce the faithful heart !
Our sins have slain the Prince of Peace ;
Our sins, which caus'd His mortal smart.
With Him we vow to crucify,
Our sins which murder'd GOD shall die !

4 We nail the Old *Adam* to the tree,
Till not one breath of life remain,
But what we can present to Thee,
(To Thee whose Blood hath purg'd our stain,)
Conjoin'd to Thy great Sacrifice,
Well-pleasing in Thy Father's eyes.

5 The saved and Saviour now agree,
In closest fellowship combined ;
We grieve, and die, and live with Thee,
To Thy great Father's will resign'd ;
And GOD doth all Thy members own
One with Thyself, for ever one.

HYMN CXXXIV.

1 JESU, we know that Thou hast died,
    And share the death we shew;
If the firstfruits be sanctified,
    The lump is holy too.

2 The sheaf was wav'd before the Lord
    When Jesus bow'd His head;
And we who thus His death record
    One with Himself are made.

3 The sheaf and harvest is but one
    Accepted Sacrifice,
And we who have Thy sufferings known,
    Shall in Thy life arise.

4 Still all-involv'd in God we are,
    And offer'd with the Lamb,
Till all in heaven with Christ appear
    Eternally the same.

HYMN CXXXV.

1 AMAZING love to mortals shew'd!
    The sinless Body of our God
Was fasten'd to the tree;

And shall our sinful members live?
No, LORD, they shall not Thee survive;
  They all shall die with Thee.

2 The feet which did to evil run,
The hands which violent acts have done,
  The greedy heart and eyes,
Base weapons of iniquity,
We offer up to death with Thee,
  A whole burnt-sacrifice.

3 Our sins are on Thine Altar laid,
We do not for their being plead,
  Or circumscribe Thy power:
Bound on Thy Cross Thou seest them lie:
Let all this cursed Adam die,
  Die, and revive no more.

4 Root out the seeds of pride and lust,
That each may of Thy Passion boast,
  Which doth the freedom give,
The world to me is crucified,
And I who on His Cross have died
  To GOD for ever live.

HYMN CXXXVI.

1 O THOU holy Lamb Divine,
    How canst Thou and sinners join ?
God of spotless purity,
How shall man concur with Thee ;

2 Offer up one Sacrifice
Acceptable to the skies ?
What shall wretched sinners bring
Pleasing to the glorious King ?

3 Only sin we call our own,
But Thou art the darling Son ;
Thine it is our God to appease,
Him Thou dost for ever please.

4 We on Thee alone depend,
With Thy Sacrifice ascend,
Render what Thy grace hath given,
Lift our souls with Thee to heaven.

HYMN CXXXVII.

1 YE royal priests of Jesus, rise,
    And join the Daily Sacrifice ;
Join all believers in His Name
To offer up the spotless Lamb.

2 Your meat and your drink-offerings throw
  On Him who suffer'd once below,
  But ever lives with GOD above,
  To plead for us His dying love.

3 Whate'er we cast on Him alone
  Is with His great Oblation one;
  His Sacrifice doth ours sustain,
  And favour and acceptance gain.

4 On Him who all our burdens bears,
  We cast our praises and our prayers;
  Ourselves we offer up to GOD,
  Implung'd in His atoning Blood.

5 Mean are our noblest offerings,
  Poor, feeble, unsubstantial things;
  But when to Him our souls we lift,
  The Altar sanctifies the gift.

6 Our persons and our deeds aspire
  When cast into that hallow'd fire,
  Our most imperfect efforts please
  When join'd to CHRIST our Righteousness.

7 Mix'd with the sacred smoke we rise,
  The smoke of His Burnt-Sacrifice,
  By the Eternal Spirit driven
  From earth, in CHRIST, we mount to heaven.

HYMN CXXXVIII.

1 ALL praise to the LORD, all praise is His due,
   To-day is His word of promise found true;
We, we are the nations, presented to GOD,
Well pleasing oblations through JESUS's Blood.

2 Poor heathens from far to JESUS we came,
And offer'd we are to GOD thro' His name;
To GOD thro' the Spirit ourselves do we give,
And saved by the merit of JESUS we live.

HYMN CXXXIX.

1 GOD of all-redeeming grace,
   By Thy pardoning love compell'd,
Up to Thee our souls we raise,
Up to Thee our bodies yield.

2 Thou our Sacrifice receive,
Acceptable thro' Thy Son,
While to Thee alone we live,
While we die to Thee alone,

3 Just it is, and good, and right,
That we should be wholly Thine.
In Thy only will delight,
In Thy blessed service join.

4 O that every thought and word
Might proclaim how good Thou art!
HOLINESS UNTO THE LORD,
Still be written on our heart.

HYMN CXL.

1 HE dies, as now for us He dies;
That all-sufficient Sacrifice
Subsists, eternal as the Lamb,
In every time and place the same;
To all alike it co-extends,
Its saving virtue never ends.

2 He lives for us to intercede,
For us he doth this moment plead;
And all who could not see Him die
May now with faith's interior eye
Behold Him stand as slaughtered there,
And feel the answer to His prayer.

3 While now for us the Saviour prays,
Father, we humbly sue for grace;
Poor, helpless, dying victims we,
Laden with sin and misery,
His infinite atonement plead,
Ourselves presenting with our Head.

4 Assur'd we shall acceptance find,
To JESUS in oblation join'd ;
Where'er the scatter'd members look
To Him who all our sorrows took,
The saving Efflux we receive,
And quicken'd by His Passion live.

HYMN CXLI.

1 HAPPY the souls that follow'd Thee
   Lamenting to the accursed wood,
Happy who underneath the tree
Unmovable in sorrow stood,

2 When nature felt the deadly blow
By which Thy soul to GOD was driven,
Which shook with sympathetic woe
Temple, and graves, and earth, and heaven.

3 O what a time for offering up
Their souls upon Thy Sacrifice !
Who would not with Thy burden stoop,
And bow the head when JESUS dies !

4 Not all the days before or since
An hour so solemn could afford
For suffering with our bleeding Prince,
For dying with our slaughter'd LORD.

5 Yet in this Ordinance Divine
　We still the sacred load may bear ;
　And now we in Thy Offering join,
　Thy Sacramental Passion share.

6 We cast our sins into that fire
　Which did Thy Sacrifice consume,
　And every base and vain desire
　To daily crucifixion doom.

7 Thou art with all Thy members here,
　In this tremendous Mystery
　We jointly before God appear,
　To offer up ourselves with Thee.

8 True followers of our Bleeding Lamb,
　Now on Thy daily Cross we die,
　And mingled in a common flame
　Ascend triumphant to the sky.

HYMN CXLII.

1　COME, we that record
　　　The death of our Lord,
　The death let us bear,
By faithful remembrance His Sacrifice share.

2   Shall we let our God groan
      And suffer alone,
      Or to *Calvary* fly,
And nobly resolve with our Master to die?

3   His servants shall be
      With Him on the Tree;
      Where Jesus was slain,
His crucified servants shall always remain.

4   By the Cross we abide
      Where Jesus hath died:
      To all we are dead;
The members can never outlive their own Head.

5   Poor penitents we
      Expect not to see
      His glory above,
Till first we have drunk of the Cup of His Love;

6   Till first we partake
      The Cross for His sake,
      And thankfully own
The Cup of His Love and His Sorrow are one.

7   Conform'd to His death
      If we suffer beneath,
      With Him we shall know
The power of His first Resurrection below.

8　　If His death we receive,
　　His life we shall live ;
　　If His Cross we sustain,
His joy and His crown we in heaven shall gain.

HYMN CXLIII.

1 FATHER, behold I come to do
　　Thy will, I come to suffer too
　　Thy acceptable will ;
Do with me, LORD, as seems Thee good,
Dispose of this weak flesh and blood,
　　And all Thy mind fulfil.

2 Thy creature in Thy hands I am,
　Frail dust and ashes is my name ;
　　The earthen vessel use :
Mould as Thou wilt the passive clay,
But let me all Thy will obey,
　　And all Thy pleasure choose.

3 Welcome whate'er my GOD ordain !
　Afflict with poverty or pain
　　This feeble flesh of mine,
(But grant me strength to bear my load,)
I will not murmur at Thy rod,
　　Or for relief repine.

4 My spirit wound (but oh ! be near)
  With what far more than death I fear,
    The darts of keenest shame,
  Fulfill'd with more than killing smart,
  And wounded in the tenderest part,
    I still adore Thy Name.

5 Beneath Thy bruising hand I fall;
  Whate'er Thou send'st, I take it all,—
    Reproach, or pain, or loss :
  I will not for deliverance pray,
  But humbly unto death obey,
    The death of JESU's Cross.

HYMN CXLIV.

1 LET both *Jews* and *Gentiles* join,
    Friends and enemies combine,
  Vent their utmost rage on me,
  Still I look through all to Thee.

2 Humbly own it is the LORD !
  Let Him wake on me His sword :
  Lo, I bow me to Thy will ;
  Thou Thy whole design fulfil.

3 Stricken by Thine anger's rod,
  Dumb I fall before my GOD,
  Or my dear Chastiser bless,
  Sing the Paschal Psalm of Praise.

4 While the bitter herbs I eat,
   Him I for my foes entreat ;
   Let me die, but oh ! forgive,
   Let my pardon'd murderers live.

HYMN CXLV.

1 FATHER, into Thy hands alone
   I have my all restor'd ;
My all Thy property I own,
   The steward of the LORD.

2 Hereafter none can take away
   My life, or goods, or fame ;
Ready at Thy demand to lay
   Them down I always am.

3 Confiding in Thy only love
   Thro' Him who died for me,
I wait Thy faithfulness to prove,
   And give back all to Thee.

4 Take when Thou wilt into Thy Hands,
   And as Thou wilt require ;
Resume by the *Sabean* bands,
   Or the devouring fire.

5 Determin'd all Thy will to obey,
   Thy blessings I restore;
Give, Lord, or take Thy gifts away,
   I praise Thee evermore.

HYMN CXLVI.

1 FATHER, if Thou willing be,
   Then my griefs awhile suspend,
Then remove the cup from me,
Or Thy strengthening angel send;
Wouldst Thou have me suffer on?
Father, let Thy will be done.

2 Let my flesh be troubled still,
   Fill'd with pain or sore disease,
Let my wounded spirit feel
Strong redoubled agonies,
Meekly I my will resign,
Thine be done, and only Thine.

3 Patient as my great High-Priest
In His bitterness of pain,
Most abandon'd and distrest,
Father, I the cross sustain:
All into Thy hands I give,
Let me die or let me live.

4 Following where my LORD hath led,
  Thee I on the Cross adore,
  Humbly bow like Him my head, ·
  All Thy benefits restore,
  Till my spirit I resign
  Breath'd into the hands Divine.

HYMN CXLVII.

1 JESU, to Thee in faith we look,
  O that our services might rise
  Perfum'd and mingled with the smoke
  Of Thy sweet-smelling Sacrifice!

2 Thy Sacrifice with heavenly powers
  Replete, all-holy, all-divine:
  Human, and weak, and sinful ours;
  How can the two oblations join?

3 Thy Offering doth to ours impart
  Its righteousness and saving grace,
  While charg'd with all our sins Thou art,
  To death devoted in our place.

4 Our mean imperfect sacrifice
  On Thine is as a burthen thrown,
  Both in a common flame arise,
  And both in GOD's account are one.

HYMN CXLVIII.

1 FATHER of mercies, hear
  Thro' Thine atoning Son,
Who doth for us in heaven appear,
 And prays before Thy throne;

2 By that great Sacrifice
  Which He for us doth plead,
Into our Saviour's death baptize,
 And make us like our Head.

3 Into the fellowship
  Of Jesu's sufferings take
Us who desire with Him to sleep,
 That we with Him may wake:

4 Plant us into His death,
  That we His life may prove,
Partakers of His Cross beneath,
 And of His Crown above.

HYMN CXLIX.

1 JESU, my strength and hope,
  My righteousness and power,
My soul is lifted up
Thy mercy to implore;

My hands I still stretch out to Thee,
My hands I fasten to the tree.

2   No more may they offend,
But do Thy work below;
Thou know'st I fain would spend
My life Thy praise to shew;
Nor will Thy gracious love despise
A sinner's meanest sacrifice.

3   Thy Wounds have wounded me,
Thy bloody Cross subdu'd;
I feel my misery,
And ever gasp for GOD;
My prayers, and griefs, and groans I join,
And mingle all my pangs with Thine.

4   JESU, a soul receive,
Upon Thine Altar cast,
To die with Thee and live
When all my deaths are past;
To live where grief can never rise,
To reign with Thee above the skies.

HYMN CL.

1 FATHER, on us the Spirit bestow,
    Thro' which Thine everlasting Son
Offer'd Himself for man below,
That *we*, e'en *we*, before Thy throne
Our souls and bodies may present,
And pay Thee all Thy grace hath lent.

2 O let Thy Spirit sanctify
Whate'er to Thee we now restore,
And make us with Thy will comply,
With all our mind, and soul, and power;
Obey Thee as Thy saints above
In perfect innocence and love.

HYMN CLI.

1 COME, Thou Spirit of contrition,
    Fill our souls with tender fears;
Conscious of our lost condition,
    Melt us into gracious tears.
Just and holy detestation
    Of our bosom sins impart, ·
Sins that caus'd our Saviour's Passion,
    Sins that stabb'd Him to the heart.

2 Fill our flesh with killing anguish,
    All our members crucify;
Let the offending nature languish
    Till on JESU's Cross it die.
All our sins to death deliver,
    Let not one, not one survive;
Then we live to GOD for ever,
    Then in heaven on earth we live.

HYMN CLII.

1 ARM of the LORD, whose vengeance laid
    My sins upon my Saviour's head;
In mercy now the sinner see,
And oh! destroy them all in me.

2 Accept, all-gracious as Thou art,
Accept a mournful sinner's heart,
Who pour my tears before my GOD
As a poor victim doth his Blood.

3 My feeble soul would fain aspire,
Its zeal, and thoughts, and whole desire
Lift up to Thee through JESU's Name,
As a burnt-sacrifice its flame.

4 And since it cannot please alone,
Accept it, Father, through Thy Son;
Supported by His Sacrifice,
Oh may it from His Altar rise.

5 Cloth'd in His righteousness receive,
  And bid me one with JESUS live ;
  Join all He sanctifies in one,
  One cross, one glory, and one crown.

HYMN CLIII.

1 FATHER, Thy feeble children meet,
    And make Thy faithful mercies known ;
  Give us through faith the Flesh to eat,
  And drink the Blood of CHRIST Thy Son.
  Honour Thine own mysterious ways,
  Thy Sacramental Presence shew,
  And all the fulness of Thy grace,
  With JESUS, on our souls bestow.

2 Father, our sacrifice receive ;
  Our souls and bodies we present,
  Our goods, and vows, and praises give,
  Whate'er Thy bounteous love hath lent.
  Thou canst not now our gift despise,
  Cast on that all-atoning Lamb,
  Mix'd with that bleeding Sacrifice,
  And offer'd up through JESU's Name.

HYMN CLIV.

1　JESU, did they crucify
　　　Thee by highest heaven ador'd?
　　Let us also go and die
　　With our dearest dying LORD.

2　LORD, Thou seest our willing heart,
　　Know'st its uppermost desire
　　With our nature's life to part,
　　Meekly on Thy Cross to expire.

3　Fain we would be all like Thee,
　　Suffer with our LORD beneath:
　　Grant us full conformity,
　　Plunge us deep into Thy death.

4　Now inflict the mortal pain,
　　Now exert Thy Passion's power;
　　Let the Man of Sin be slain,
　　Die the flesh to live no more.

HYMN CLV.

1　FATHER, SON, and HOLY GHOST,
　　　One in Three, and Three in One,
　　As by the celestial host
　　Let Thy will on earth be done;

Praise by all to Thee be given,
Glorious LORD of earth and heaven !

2 Vilest of the fallen race,
Lo, I answer to Thy call ;
Meanest vessel of Thy grace
(Grace divinely free for all),
Lo, I come to do Thy will,
All Thy counsel to fulfil.

3 If so poor a worm as I
May to Thy great glory live,
All my actions sanctify,
All my words and thoughts receive ;
Claim me for Thy service, claim
All I have and all I am.

4 Take my soul and body's powers,
Take my memory, mind, and will,
All my goods, and all my hours,
All I know, and all I feel,
All I think, and speak, and do,—
Take my heart, but make it new.

5 Now, O GOD, Thine own I am,
Now I give Thee back Thy own ;
Freedom, friends, and health, and fame,
Consecrate to Thee alone :
Thine I live, thrice happy I,
Happier still for Thine I die.

6 FATHER, SON, and HOLY GHOST,
  One in Three, and Three in One,
  As by the celestial host
  Let Thy will on earth be done ;
  Praise by all to Thee be given,
  Glorious LORD of earth and heaven !

HYMN CLVI.

1   ALL glory and praise
        To the Ancient of Days,
  Who was born and was slain to redeem a lost race.

2   Salvation to GOD,
     Who carried our load,
  And purchas'd our lives with the price of His
        Blood.

3   And shall He not have
     The lives which He gave
  Such an infinite ransom for ever to save ?

4   Yes, LORD, we are Thine,
     And gladly resign
  Our souls to be fill'd with the fulness Divine.

5   We yield Thee Thine own,
     We serve Thee alone ;
  Thy will upon earth as in heaven be done.

6   How, when it shall be
    We cannot foresee;
 But, oh, let us live, let us die unto Thee!

HYMN CLVII.

1 LET Him to whom we now belong
   His sovereign right assert,
 And take up every thankful song,
   And every loving heart.

2 He justly claims us for His own
   Who bought us with a price;
 The Christian lives to *Christ* alone,
   To *Christ* alone He dies.

3 JESU, Thine own at last receive,
   Fulfil our hearts' desire,
 And let us to Thy glory live,
   And in Thy cause expire.

4 Our souls and bodies we resign;
   With joy we render Thee
 Our all, no longer ours, but Thine,
   Through all eternity.

VI. *After the* SACRAMENT.

HYMN CLVIII.

1

ALL praise to God above,
  In whom we have believ'd,
The token of whose dying love
  We have e'en now receiv'd:

2   Have with His Flesh been fed,
     And drank His precious Blood;
His precious Blood is Drink indeed,
     His Flesh immortal Food.

3   O what a taste is this
     Which now in *Christ* we know,
An earnest of our glorious bliss,
     Our heaven begun below!

4   When He the Table spreads,
     How royal is the cheer!
With rapture we lift up our heads,
     And own that God is here.

5   He bids us taste His grace,
       The joys of angels prove:
The stammerers' tongues are loos'd to praise
       Our dear Redeemer's love.

6   Salvation to our GOD
       That sits upon the throne;
Salvation be alike bestow'd
       On His triumphant Son!

7   The Lamb for sinners slain,
       Who died to die no more,
Let all the ransom'd sons of men
       With all His hosts adore:

8   Let earth and heaven be join'd,
       His glories to display,
And hymn the Saviour of mankind
       In one eternal day.

HYMN CLIX.

1 ALL glory and praise to JESUS our LORD!
    His ransoming grace we gladly record,
His bloody Oblation, and death on the tree
Hath purchas'd salvation and heaven for me.

2 The Saviour hath died for *me* and for *you*,
The Blood is applied, the record is true;
The Spirit bears witness, and speaks in the Blood,
And gives us the fitness for living with GOD.

HYMN CLX.

1 WELCOME, delicious, sacred cheer;
    Welcome, my GOD, my Saviour dear!
  O with me, in me, live and dwell!
Thine earthly joy surpasses quite,
The depths of Thy supreme delight
  Not angel-tongues can fully tell.

2 What streams of sweetness from the bowl
Surprise and deluge all my soul,
    Sweetness which is, and makes divine!
Surely from GOD's right hand they flow,
From thence derive to earth below,
    To cheer us with immortal Wine.

3 Soon as I taste the heavenly Bread,
What manna o'er my soul is shed,
    Manna that angels never knew!
Victorious sweetness fills my heart,
Such as my GOD delights to impart,
    Mighty to save, and sin subdue.

4 I had forgot my heavenly birth,
My soul degenerate clave to earth,
    In sense and sin's base pleasures drown'd,
When God assum'd humanity,
And spilt His sacred Blood for me,
    To wash, and lift me from the ground.

5 Soon as His love has rais'd me up,
He mingles blessings in a cup,
    And sweetly meets my ravish'd taste;
Joyous I now throw off my load,
I cast my sins and care on God,
    And wine becomes a wing at last.

6 Upborne on this, I mount, I fly;
Regaining swift my native sky,
    I wipe my streaming eyes, and see
Him whom I seek, for whom I sue;
My God, my Saviour, there I view,
    And live with Him who died for me.

HYMN CLXI.

"Therefore with Angels and Archangels," etc.

1 LORD and God of heavenly powers,
    Theirs—yet oh! benignly ours;
Glorious King, let earth proclaim,
Worms attempt to chant Thy Name.

2 Thee to laud in songs divine,
  Angels and archangels join ;
  We with them our voices raise,
  Echoing Thy eternal praise.

3 Holy, holy, holy LORD,
  Live by heaven and earth ador'd !
  Full of Thee they ever cry,
  Glory be to GOD most high !

HYMN CLXII.

1 HOSANNA in the highest,
      To our exalted Saviour,
  Who left behind
  For all mankind
  These Tokens of His favour.

2 His bleeding love and mercy,
  His all-redeeming Passion,
      Who here displays
      And gives the grace
  Which brings us our salvation.

3 Louder than gather'd waters,
  Or bursting peals of thunder,
      We lift our voice,
      And speak our joys,
  And shout our loving wonder !

4 Shout, all our elder brethren,
    While we record the story
        Of Him that came,
        And suffer'd shame
    To carry us to glory.

5 Angels in fix'd amazement
    Around our Altars hover,
        With eager gaze
        Adore the grace
    Of our eternal Lover :

6 Himself, and all His fulness,
    Who gives to the believer ;
        And by this Bread
        Whoe'er are fed
    Shall live with GOD for ever !

HYMN CLXIII.

"Glory be to GOD on high, and on earth peace," etc.

1 GLORY be to GOD on high,
    GOD, whose glory fills the sky ;
Peace on earth to man forgiven,
Man, the well-belov'd of heaven !

2 Sovereign Father, heavenly King,
Thee we now presume to sing;
Glad Thine attributes confess,
Glorious all, and numberless.

3 Hail by all Thy works ador'd,
Hail the everlasting LORD!
Thee with thankful hearts we prove,
LORD of power, and GOD of love.

4 CHRIST our LORD and GOD we own,
CHRIST, the Father's only Son;
Lamb of GOD for sinners slain,
Saviour of offending man.

5 Bow Thine ear, in mercy bow,
Hear the world's Atonement Thou:
JESU, in Thy name we pray,
Take, O take our sins away.

6 Powerful Advocate with GOD,
Justify us by Thy Blood!
Bow Thine ear, in mercy bow,
Hear the world's Atonement Thou!

7 Hear; for Thou, O CHRIST, alone
With Thy glorious Sire art One,
One the Holy Ghost with Thee,
One supreme Eternal Three!

M

HYMN CLXIV.

1 SONS of GOD, triumphant rise,
  Shout the accomplish'd Sacrifice,
  Shout your sins in CHRIST forgiven,
  Sons of GOD and heirs of heaven !

2 Ye that round our Altars throng,
  Listening angels, join the song ;
  Sing with us, ye heavenly powers,
  Pardon, grace, and glory ours !

3 Love's mysterious work is done ;
  Greet we now the atoning Son :
  Heal'd and quicken'd by His Blood,
  Join'd to CHRIST, and one with GOD.

4 CHRIST, of all our hopes the seal ;
  Peace Divine in CHRIST we feel ;
  Pardon to our souls applied ;
  Dead for all, for *me* He died.

5 Sin shall tyrannize no more,
  Purg'd its guilt, dissolv'd its power ;
  JESUS makes our hearts His throne,
  There He lives and reigns alone.

6 Grace our every thought controls,
  Heaven is open'd in our souls,
  Everlasting life is won,
  Glory is on earth begun.

7 CHRIST in us; in Him we see
  Fulness of the Deity,
  Beam of the Eternal Beam;
  Life Divine we taste in Him.

8 Him by faith we taste below,
  Mightier joys ordain'd to know,
  When His utmost grace we prove,
  Rise to heaven by Perfect Love.

HYMN CLXV.

1 HOW happy are Thy servants, LORD,
    Who thus remember Thee!
  What tongue can tell our sweet accord,
    Our perfect harmony?

2 Who Thy mysterious Supper share,
    Here at Thy Table fed,
  Many, and yet but one we are,
    One undivided Bread.

3 One with the Living Bread Divine,
    Which now by faith we eat;
  Our hearts, and minds, and spirits join,
    And all in JESUS meet.

4 So dear the tie where souls agree
   In JESU's dying love:
Then only can it closer be
   When all are join'd above.

HYMN CLXVI.

1 HAPPY the saints of former days
   Who first continued in the Word,
A simple, lowly, loving race,
   True followers of their lamb-like LORD.

2 In holy fellowship they liv'd,
   Nor would from the commandment move,
But every joyful day received
   The Tokens of expiring love.

3 Not then above their Master wise,
   They simply in His paths remain'd ;
And call'd to mind His Sacrifice
   With steadfast faith and love unfeign'd.

4 From house to house they broke the Bread
   Impregnated with Life Divine,
And drank the Spirit of their Head
   Transmitted in the sacred Wine.

5 With JESU's constant Presence blest,
  While duteous to His dying word,
  They kept the Eucharistic Feast,
  And supp'd in *Eden* with their LORD.

6 Throughout their spotless lives was seen
  The virtue of this heavenly Food;
  Superior to the sons of men,
  They soar'd aloft, and walk'd with GOD.

7 O what a flame of sacred love
  Was kindled by the Altar's fire!
  They lived on earth like those above,
  Glad rivals of the heavenly choir.

8 Strong in the strength herewith receiv'd,
  And mindful of the Crucified,
  His confessors for Him they liv'd,
  For Him His faithful martyrs died.

9 Their souls from chains of flesh releas'd,
  By torture from their bodies driven,
  With violent faith the kingdom seiz'd,
  And fought and forc'd their way to heaven.

10 Where is the pure primeval flame
  Which in their faithful bosom glow'd?
  Where are the followers of the Lamb,
  The dying witnesses for God?

11   Why is the faithful seed decreas'd,
The life of GOD extinct and dead?
The Daily Sacrifice is ceas'd,
And charity to heaven is fled.

12   Sad mutual causes of decay,
Slackness and vice together move ;
Grown cold we cast the means away,
And quench'd the latest spark of love.

13   The sacred Signs Thou didst ordain,
Our pleasant things, are all laid waste ;
To men of lips and hearts profane,
To dogs and swine and heathens cast.

14   Thine holy Ordinance contemn'd
Hath let the flood of evil in,
And those who by Thy Name are nam'd,
The sinners unbaptiz'd outsin.

15   But canst Thou not Thy work revive
Once more in our degenerate years?
O wouldst Thou with Thy rebels strive,
And melt them into gracious tears !

16   O wouldst Thou to Thy Church return !
For which the faithful remnant sighs,
For which the drooping nations mourn ;
Restore the Daily Sacrifice.

17 Return, and with Thy servants sit,
    Lord of the Sacramental Feast,
    And satiate us with heavenly Meat,
    And make the *world* Thy happy guest.

18 Now let the Spouse, reclin'd on Thee,
    Come up out of the wilderness,
    From every spot and wrinkle free,
    And wash'd and perfected in grace.

19 Thou hear'st the pleading Spirit's groan,
    Thou know'st the groaning Spirit's will:
    Come in Thy gracious kingdom down,
    And all Thy ransom'd servants seal.

20 Come quickly, Lord, the Spirit cries,
    The number of Thy saints complete;
    Come quickly, Lord, the Bride replies,
    And make us all for glory meet.

21 Erect Thy tabernacle here,
    The *New Jerusalem* send down;
    Thyself amidst Thy saints appear,
    And seat us on Thy dazzling Throne.

22 Begin the great Millennial Day;
    Now, Saviour, with a shout descend;
    Thy standard in the heavens display,
    And bring the joy which ne'er shall end.

INDEX.

Beginning with the First Line of every Hymn.

J.

L.

O.

CHISWICK PRESS:—CHARLES WHITTINGHAM, TOOKS COURT,
CHANCERY LANE.

JOHN HODGES'
LIST OF PUBLICATIONS.

By W. CHATTERTON DIX.

Vision of All Saints, and other Poems.   Crown
8vo., handsomely bound, 2*s.* 6*d.*   Second Edition.   Dedicated
by permission to the Lord Chancellor.

> "Mr. Dix is a real sacred poet.   His verses are not merely graceful, but true poetry.   We have seldom read more stately and triumphant lines than his Expectant Bride and Processional for Ascension-tide."—*Sacristy.*

> "The volume contains many beauties, which remind a reader of the best productions of Keble, and of the old Catholic poets, Southwell and Crawshaw."—*Weekly Register.*

The Pilgrims of the Passion.   Square 32mo., 1*d.*

The Litany of the Good Shepherd.   Set to Music
by J. D. SEDDING, ½*d.*, or 3*s.* 6*d.* per 100.

The Days of First Love.   A Poem.   32mo., 3*d.*

Altar Songs: Verses on the Holy Eucharist.
Second Edition, enlarged.   16mo., 6*d.*

Come to the Woods, and other Poems.   By the
Rev. G. J. CORNISH, M.A., late Vicar of Kenwyn-with-
Kea, and Prebendary of Exeter.   Fcap. 8vo., 2*s.* 6*d.*   New
Edition.

> "It is a true volume of fancy, and the fancy is marked by tenderness and purity.   All the poems are short ; some of them like sweet cabinet pictures, found not in exhibitions, but occasionally in some friend's house, and always looked at with love and admiration."—*Nonconformist.*

JOHN HODGES' NEW LIST.

The Official Report of the Church Congress, held at Swansea, October the 6th, 7th, 8th, and 9th, 1879. President, the Right Rev. WM. BASIL JONES, D.D., Lord Bishop of St. David's. Edited by the Rev. F. W. EDMONDS, M.A., Vicar of Bridgend. Demy 8vo., cloth, 10*s.* 6*d.*

The Sermons Preached on the Day of the Opening of the Congress, at the Parish Church by His Grace the ARCHBISHOP OF CANTERBURY, and at Holy Trinity Church by the LORD BISHOP OF WINCHESTER. 8vo., sewed, 1*s.*

Historical Portraits of the Tudor Dynasty and the Reformation Period. By S. HUBERT BURKE. Vol. I., demy 8vo., 550 pp., 15*s.* To be completed in Three Volumes. Vol. II. nearly ready.

" Time unveils all truth."

Extract from a letter to the Author by the Right Hon. W. E. GLADSTONE, M.P. :—"I have read every page of the work with great interest, and I subscribe without hesitation to the eulogy passed on it by the ' Daily Chronicle,' as making, *as far as I know, a distinct and valuable addition to our knowledge of a remarkable period.*"

Readings, Meditations, and Hymns for the Sick. Fcap. 8vo., limp cloth, red edges, 1*s.* 6*d.*

Wesley's Altar Manual. Being the Eucharistic Manuals and Hymns of JOHN and CHARLES WESLEY. Reprinted from the Original Editions. Edited, with a Preface, by W. E. DUTTON, Vicar of Menstone. Cloth, red edges, bevelled boards, 2*s.* 6*d.* *[Just ready.*

Church or Dissent? An Appeal to Holy Scripture (addressed to Dissenters). By T. P. GARNIER, M.A., Rector of Cranworth with Southburgh, Norfolk, and late Fellow of All Souls' College, Oxford. Crown 8vo., cloth, 2*s*. 6*d*. Sixth Thousand.

Moral and Religious Estimate of Vivisection (reprinted from "The Gentleman's Magazine"). By HENRY N. OXENHAM, M.A. 8vo., 6*d*.

Herder's Scripture Prints. Forty Coloured Pictures Illustrating the Old and New Testament. Very suitable for Schools or Cottages. Price 12*s*. the set, or mounted and varnished, price £2 2*s*.

*** A fresh supply just received.*

Stories on the Creed. By ELLEN LIPSCOMBE. Uniform with "Sunday Festival and Bible Stories."

[*In the press.*

John Wesley in Company with High Churchmen. Crown 8vo., cloth, Sixth and Cheaper Edition, Revised and Enlarged, 2*s*. 6*d*. ; limp cloth, 1*s*. 6*d*.

Faith and Duty. By the Editors of "The Gospeller." Crown 8vo., cloth, 3*s*. 6*d*. ; or in Three Parts, 1*s*. each.

CONTENTS :—Elementary Instructions in Church Principles, Hints for Daily Life, Days and Seasons, &c.

Priestcraft and Progress. Lectures and Sermons by STEWART D. HEADLAM, B.A., late Curate of Bethnal Green. Price 2*s*. 6*d*., post-free.

"Our advice to the clergy and laity is to get this book, read it, preach it, and live by it."—*Church Times.*

By C. A. JONES,

Author of " Our Childhood's Pattern," &c.

Sunday and Festival Stories. This Popular Series
may be had in the following form :—

13 Packets at 1s. each.

Any Parts or Vols. may be had separately.

A New Edition in 6 Vols., 2s. 6d. each.

"The tales are appropriate, interesting, and well adapted for reading to
children in our Sunday-schools."—*Church Opinion.*

"All these are not only good, but are also the kind of thing which will
be read, and we advise those of our readers who are looking out for this
kind of literature to get them."—*Literary Churchman.*

"They are brief and plain, pointing out distinctly and clearly the moral
of the day, serving excellently to bring out the meaning of the services,
and though of course they are marked by a decided Church feeling, they
contain nothing extreme or intolerant."—*Guardian.*

How Rachel Lee found the Christmas Gift.
Price 6d.

Little Ones at Home. With Thirty Illustrations.
Cloth extra, 2s.

Bible Stories for Children and Schools. Square
16mo, cloth, 2s. 6d. ; or in 3 parts, 1s. each.

Lights and Shadows. Stories of Every-day Life.
Two parts, each containing five Stories, price 6d. each.

Churchman's Sixpenny Library, The. A Series
of Devotional, Practical, and Doctrinal Works, suitable for circulation among Churchmen. Consisting of Translations, Selections from the Standard English Divines, and Original Works. Each post free for 7 stamps.

Vol. 1. The Imitation of Christ. 300 pages.

Vol. 2. The Spiritual Combat.

Vol. 3. The Rule of Faith.

Vol. 4. The Narrow Way.

Vol. 5 and 6. Daily Text Book for the Christian Year.

In One Vol., limp cloth, 1s.; roan, 2s. 6d.

Vol. 7. The Life of God in the Soul of Man.

Vol. 8. A Guide for passing Lent Holily. From the French of Avrillon.

Vol. 9. The Inner Life ; or, the Spiritual Guidance in the Ways of God. From the French of the Abbé Baudrand.

Vol. 10. A Guide for passing Advent Holily. From the French of Avrillon.

Vol. 11. The Rule of Life. By the Author of "The Rule of Faith."

Vol. 12. Notes on the Book of Common Prayer; being a Companion Volume to "The Narrow Way."

Vol. 13. The Rule of Prayer. By the Author of "The Rule of Faith," and "The Rule of Life." [*In the Press.*

Any of the above may be had in limp roan, with outline Cross on the cover, price 1s. 6d., or in limp calf, 2s. 6d.

"Complaints were made some time ago through our columns of the dearness of Church publications. Let us impress upon Churchmen the duty of supporting this attempt to provide first-rate publications at a cheap price. Only a very large sale will justify the continuance of the scheme ; we may think ourselves well off with editions so thoroughly readable as these at 6d."—*Church Review.*

PEOPLE.

HODGES' CHRISTIAN CLASSICS.

Under the above title it is intended to issue and continue the Series known as the " Churchman's Shilling Library."

It is proposed to reproduce specimens of Popular Christian Literature, consisting of translations and selections from the works of Standard Divines of all ages. The Series will include Christian Evidences, History, Biography, and Devotion ; and an attempt will be made to familiarize English readers with some of the works which have instructed and interested every section of the Catholic Church.

The Series will be issued monthly, in demy 16mo, limp cloth, price 1*s.* each.

Among the earlier volumes will be—" St. Cyprian on the Lord's Prayer," " Lacordaire's Letters to Young Men," " The Banquet of the Ten Virgins," " The Pastor of Hermas " (a very popular work of the second century), " Hall's Meditations," " Some Ancient Christian Martyrologies," " St. Augustine on the City of God," " Cave's Primitive Christians," " Counsels from Fénélon," " Beveridge on Christian Life," &c. &c.

CHRISTIAN CLASSICS.

Vols. 1 and 4 in one vol., cloth, red edges, 2s. 6d.

Vols. 12 and 13 in one vol., 2s. 6d.

Vols. 1, 2, 4, 5, and 6, limp persian, 2s. 6d.; calf or morocco, 5s.

Several others Preparing.

By the Rev. H. W. HOLDEN.

John Wesley in Company with High Church-

men. Crown 8vo., cloth, price 4s. Fifth Edition. Revised and Enlarged.

Amongst the additional matter, which amounts to nearly one-fourth of the original work, will be found the maintenance by Wesley and the early Methodists of " Religious Houses," Spiritual Retreats, Mortuary Celebrations, the Daily Eucharist, &c., &c., and his own disavowal of his conversion in 1738.

Opinions of the Press.

"A very strong, if not a complete, identity of view is established between the great Church Reformer of the last century and the Ritual Revivers of the present century."—*Irish Church Society's Journal.*

"The various quotations given from Mr. Wesley's works are so contrary to what has been the general opinion of his belief, and at the same time so well authenticated, that the book should be carefully studied by every Churchman and every Wesleyan who wishes to arrive at an unprejudiced opinion."—*Church Opinion.*

"A book like this ought to settle the question between the Church and the Methodists."—*Literary Churchman.*

"It entirely destroys the fiction of the Wesleyans that their founder was a High Churchman only up to the date he called his conversion."—*English Churchman.*

Cheaper issue, price 3d.

The Wesleyan Controversy. A Correspondence

between JAMES H. RIGG, D.D., Principal of the Wesleyan Training College, Westminster, and H. W. HOLDEN, Curate of Grasby, Brigg, Lincoln.

"Well worth reprinting. The Correspondence is very diverting. But it is valuable as well."—*The Literary Churchman.*

Tenth Thousand, price 4d.

The Children's Hymnal and Christian Year,

for Use at Children's Services. Edited by the Rev. C. H. BATEMAN, Vicar of Child's Hill, Middlesex, Author of "Hymns and Melodies for Schools and Families."

A Manual of School Prayers, Litanies, and

Form of Children's Services. By THEODORE JOHNSON, C.M.D., Master of All Saints' School, Bingham, Notts. 16mo., price 6d.

Simple Hymns for Little Children. By E. C. W.

Royal 16mo., price 6d.

Six Books for Rewards, School Prizes, &c.

Price 6d. each.

> The Garden by the River; or, the Children of the Church. An Allegory.
>
> Bertha's Dream, and other Tales.
>
> Golden Opportunities. Two Short Tales.
>
> Ellen's Baptism; or, Do let me be Christened.
>
> Roger Arnold; or, The Sunday Class.
>
> A Storm on the Lake of Lucerne. From the German.

THE GOLDEN GATE.

By the Rev. S. BARING-GOULD, M.A.

A COMPLETE MANUAL OF INSTRUCTIONS, DEVOTIONS, AND PREPARATIONS.

New Edition, in 1 vol., cloth, 2s. 6d.

"We pronounce this to be a book which will impart to the reader a clearer understanding of the Holy Catholic Faith *in extenso*, in all its subtle ramifications, its mysteries, its ceremonies, its demands upon the heart and the intellect, than any work of the kind that has ever been published. Simple in language, apposite in illustration, earnest in purpose. it addresses itself to all classes of readers—to Catholics as a guide, to Protestants as a light."—*Leader.*

"It has all the clearness and clever condensed incisiveness of his usua. style, and we have scarcely ever seen so small a book with so much solid material in it. There is scarcely a superfluous word. It may be described as general instructions on doctrine and practice, together with a clever sketch of Church History, and some clever and telling answers to popular objections against religion."—*Literary Churchman.*

"The devotions it contains are suited to every variety. of circumstances in which any individual may be placed. It only professes to be a compilation for the use of devout laity living in the world ; but we heartily thank Mr. Baring-Gould for it as an excellent and convenient book of devotions, which, when derived from foreign sources, are rendered in thorough good English. The instructions are done in a popular and attractive style, with much vigour and originality."—*Church Herald.*

"The best praise we can give the book is to say that it exactly fulfils the condition of the title-page, being golden in quality, and complete in the quantity, variety, and scope of the instructions and devotions which it provides. It may be briefly described as a spiritual storehouse, which contains something of everything likely to be wanted by a devout Catholic. . . . . . We do not hesitate to place 'The Golden Gate,' for fulness and lucidity, at the head of all our devotional manuals, and as such to recommend it cordially to our readers."—*Church Review.*

Our Curate's Budget.

Edited by the Rev. W. MICHELL, M.A.   The series is now complete in 120 Nos. at 3*d.* each, or 20 Volumes, cloth with Frontispiece, 2*s.* each.

No.
 1. Tom Edwards.
 2. My Two Sick Friends.
 3. True-Hearted, Long-Parted.
 4. Black Brian.
 5. Ben the Barge Boy.
 6. The New Vicar.
 7. The Two Baptisms.
 8. Sister's Children.
 9. Susan's First Place.
10. S. Michael's.
11. William Baird.
12. Blue Anchor Yard.
13. Ash Tree Turnpike.
14. Agatha's Working-day.
15. The Broad-lane Tea Party.
16. Crofton Cricket Club.
17. Dismissed from the Choir.
18. Fustian Jenny.
19. Harry Mason's Repentance.
20. Cloud and Sunshine.
21. Silver or Pewter.
22. William Fisher's Lesson.
23. An Old Score.
24. Out of his Time.
25. Gilbert Lorimer's Vow.
26. Martin's Common.
27. So very Genteel.
28. Peppery Mike.
29. Mary's Sacrifice.
30. Coals of Fire.
31. A Dangerous Gift.
32. Better than Rubies.
33. A Changeful Life.
34. Time Enough.
35. The Miller of Basildon.
36. The Stranger at Heathcote.
37. From Treble to Tenor.
38. Old Molly.
39. Gentlefolks Once.
40. Husband and Wife.
41. The Dictation Prize.
42. The Prayers of the Church.
43. Lightly Spoken.
44. The Best Girl in the Place.

No.
45. Mary Deane's Trial.
46. Not to be Daunted.
47. Polly's First Earnings.
48. Crippled Donald.
49. Most Haste, Worst Speed.
50. The Plague of the Village.
51. Cousin Esther's Bible.
52. An Aggrieved Parishioner.
53. Sound Root, Good Fruit.
54. Under the Stars.
55. Shadow and Substance.
56. Up in the Black Country.
57. Raw Material.
58. A Rise in Life.
59. The Gate of Heaven.
60. Turned Adrift.
61. The Widower's Home.
62. Godfather George.
63. Next Door Neighbours.
64. Troubles Past, Safe at Last.
65. Across the Atlantic.
66. John Coverdale's Right Hand.
67. The Foster Brothers.
68. Getting or Saving.
69. Charlie's Last Lesson.
70. Pierre Gautier's Story.
71. For Her Boy's Sake.
72. Webber the Quartermaster.
73. A New Leaf.
74. Perkin's Court.
75. Needles and Spades.
76. The Chorister's Window.
77. Lucie's Faith.
78. A Pretty Kettle of Fish.
79. Rasoa.
80. Divided by Tens.
81. Peggy's Guiding Star.
82. All His Own Fault.
83. Who Did It?
84. Chums.
85. Stormy Day has Bright To morrow.
86. Better Days.
87. Strife and Peace in Horram.

Our Curate's Budget—*continued.*

No.
- 88. Susannah's Good Friday.
- 89. Quite a Low Boy.
- 90. Green House *v.* Green Man.
- 91. Ragged Robin.
- 92. Hasty Wooing, Bitter Ruing.
- 93. A Long Watch.
- 94. Widow Tom.
- 95. Milicent's Wedding.
- 96. Peace on Earth.
- 97. From Death to Life.
- 98. Not Wanted Here.
- 99. She Would have her Way.
- 100. To School at Last.
- 101. Keep your own Place.
- 102. Because it's the Fashion.
- 103. Soldier and Servant.
- 104. The Better Country.

No.
- 105. Overlooked.
- 106. The Clock and the Choir.
- 107. Under the Hedge.
- 108. The Last of the Year.
- 109. Fast Friends.
- 110. Uncle Jack.
- 111. For the Truth's Sake.
- 112. The Confirmation at Maberley.
- 113. The Turn of the Tide.
- 114. My God-daughter Agnes.
- 115. Nellie's Work for God.
- 116. Two Prices.
- 117. Margaret's Love Story.
- 118. The Babes in the Wheat.
- 119. Squatters' Heath.
- 120. In Two Homes.

"There is a thorough manly tone about them; they are free from cant or sensation, and what is equally objectionable, the extreme goodness of too many of this class of stories. There should not be a school library, servants' hall, soldiers' barracks, or ship's cabin without a set. They also suit admirably for distribution at missions. Our only regret is that the sale is not ten times what it is; the good effect would be immense. The editor has conferred a lasting benefit on the Church, and we trust that he may long be spared to continue his work."—*The Banner.*

"It is just the Series that is wanted for distribution. Interesting tales, with a decided Church tone, yet not written so as to disgust with the least affectation of cant."—*John Bull.*

"The sensible and well told stories are specially suitable for parochial lending libraries; and we sincerely hope the respected editor may receive support and help in continuing so much needed and useful a work."—*Union Review.*

The following classification may prove useful to those using the Nos. for distribution:—

Boys—1, 5, 7, 12, 17, 19, 21, 25, 26, 28, 31, 34, 37, 41, 46, 48, 50, 54, 57, 60, 64, 69, 76, 78, 89, 91, 94, 100.

Young Men—4, 11, 13, 16, 20, 22, 24, 43, 49, 58, 82, 83, 90.

Girls and Young Women—3, 9, 14, 27, 29, 30, 32, 44, 45, 47, 51, 55, 56, 61, 77, 81, 92, 93, 99, 101.

Church Work and Doctrine—2, 6, 8, 15, 38, 42, 52, 59, 62, 71, 88, 96, 98, 102, 107.

General—10, 18, 23, 33, 35, 36, 39, 40, 53, 63, 65, 66, 67, 68, 70, 72, 73, 74, 80, 85, 86, 87, 95, 108.

Confirmation—5, 31, 57, 60, 64.

Foreign Missions—75, 79, 97.

Home Missions—84.

JOHN HODGES, 24, KING WILLIAM STREET, LONDON.

THE GOSPEL STORY.

By the Rev. W. MICHELL, M.A.,

INSPECTOR OF SCHOOLS FOR THE DIOCESE OF BATH AND WELLS.

A Plain Commentary on the Four Gospels. Containing the Narrative of our Blessed Lord's Life and Ministry. Dedicated by permission to the Rev. CANON LIDDON, D.D., D.C.L., &c.

3 vols., fcap. 8vo., cloth, 3s. 6d. each. Fourth Thousand.

"Now that the training of our future elementary schoolmasters is becoming more than ever important, we should hope that the clergy will see to it that their pupil teachers are brought from the first to understand Scripture in its true sense. For this purpose no better help could be found than 'The Gospel Story.' It ought to be found in every parish and in every school."—*Literary Church-man.*

"We would strongly recommend the book as specially suited for the use of district visitors, who are not unfrequently perplexed to know what to read to those whom they are called upon to visit."—*Church Herald.*

"This is exactly what has long been wanted, a clear, simple life of our Lord, written for those not well educated or much instructed. For putting into such hands nothing could be better."—*Sacristy.*

"A most admirable commentary on the Four Gospels."—*John Bull.*

"The utility of the book is manifest, its orthodoxy unimpeachable, its language simple, and its tone devotional."—*Church Times.*

"It is what it calls itself—a really 'Plain Commentary on the Four Gospels.' It avoids the common faults of diffusiveness and vagueness, and gives real explanation, followed by real practical application; and though the words are plain and the sentences short, the teaching is high and spiritual."—*Guardian.*

"It is just such a book as should be in all households."—*Churchman's Companion.*

SUNDAY AND FESTIVAL STORIES.

This Popular Series may be had in the following forms :—

> 13 Packets at 1*s*. each.
> 6 Volumes in handsome cloth binding, 15*s*.

Any Numbers, Parts, or Volumes may be had separately.

FROM ADVENT SUNDAY TO WHITSUN-DAY.

No.
1. The Armour of Light.
2. Old Reuben's Story.
3. The Faithful Steward.
4. Christmas Joy.
5. Tim's Inheritance.
6. The Far-off Star.
7. Slothful John.
8. Hugh's Enemy.
9. The Powers that be.
10. Until the Harvest.
11. Like unto Christ.
12. Hilton School.
13. And in time of Temptation Fall Away.
14. The Most Excellent Gift.

No.
15. Walter Grey's Abstinence.
16. Harold's Prayer.
17. A Priest's Narrative.
18. Comfort of God's Grace.
19. The Way of the Cross.
20. Mark, the Chorister.
21. Easter Light.
22. Tim's Peace.
23. Suffering Wrongfully.
24. The Mother's Last Wish.
25. The Wanderer's Home.
26. Aunt Milly's School Days.
27. Elsie's Trial.
28. A Whitsun-day at Cologne.

SUNDAY AND FESTIVAL STORIES

(continued).

TRINITY SUNDAY TO TWENTY-FIFTH SUNDAY AFTER.

<table>
<tr><td>No.</td><td></td><td>No.</td><td></td></tr>
<tr><td>1.</td><td>Our Dick.</td><td>14.</td><td>Jim Calcott's Revenge.</td></tr>
<tr><td>2.</td><td>Gentleman Jack.</td><td>15.</td><td>The Fruit of the Spirit.</td></tr>
<tr><td>3.</td><td>The Double Vow.</td><td>16.</td><td>Grace's First Thought.</td></tr>
<tr><td>4.</td><td>S. Mary's Home.</td><td>17.</td><td>What is a Cross?</td></tr>
<tr><td>5.</td><td>The Harsh Judgment.</td><td>18.</td><td>Guy's Baptism.</td></tr>
<tr><td>6.</td><td>The Old Feud.</td><td>19.</td><td>The Great Commandment.</td></tr>
<tr><td>7.</td><td>Tom Martin.</td><td>20.</td><td>Forgiving Jack.</td></tr>
<tr><td>8.</td><td>Ruth's Offering.</td><td>21.</td><td>Ready in Body and Soul.</td></tr>
<tr><td>9.</td><td>Newland Bay.</td><td>22.</td><td>The Quiet Mind.</td></tr>
<tr><td>10.</td><td>Self-Conceit.</td><td>23.</td><td>Charlie's Promise.</td></tr>
<tr><td>11.</td><td>Holy Ground.</td><td>24.</td><td>The Prayer of Faith.</td></tr>
<tr><td>12.</td><td>Humble Ned.</td><td>25.</td><td>John Noble's Repentance.</td></tr>
<tr><td>13.</td><td>Harry's Conscience.</td><td>26.</td><td>The Soft Answer.</td></tr>
</table>

"Each story is founded upon some point in the Epistle or Gospel for the day ; nothing could be better for reading to a Sunday class." *—Church Review.*

"They are short and well told, and will suit excellently for parish school use."*—Guardian.*

"Our notice of them is necessarily brief, but it is not the less emphatic. We earnestly hope that they will have a large sale. They are sure to be popular, and sure to be useful."*—Literary Churchman.*